A.N. VEREBES

Truth Hurts

Jukebox Collection Book 3

First edition

This book was professionally typeset on Reedsy.
Find out more at reedsy.com

For Mark, Sylvia and Claire.
You've supported me through my tears and temper tantrums over this one, so I would say you've definitely earned the dedication.
No, you're not getting any of the royalties. :P

Contents

Preface

Firstly, this book contains explicit content not suitable for persons under 18 years of age.

Secondly, while *Truth Hurts* is the third book in the *Jukebox Collection* series, it can be read as a standalone.

However, if you would like an ebook copy of Book 1 (*Handle With Care*) for free, you can sign up to my newsletter* via https://anverebesauthor.wordpress.com/newsletter_signup and receive a copy in pdf, mobi or epub, distributed via Dropbox (for which you don't need an account).

*Obviously, you're welcome to unsubscribe at any time, but I promise I don't send spam

Acknowledgement

This book very nearly didn't happen. Then my amazing editor, Tanya Tanaka, got her hands onto it and helped shape it into a story I'm proud to put my name to.

Tanya, you make me a better writer. I am so very lucky to have found you. Or you found me. Either way, I'm still the lucky one in this situation. Thank you for sticking with me through this. I swear Book 4 won't be as messy when I send it to you!*

*Does putting this promise to print make it legally binding?

Chapter One

"You're not serious?" Margot began before Rosie could even squeeze in a greeting. This sort of thing was typical behaviour for her editor. "I know you're scratching the bottom of the barrel for inspiration, Rose, but-"

"Hello to you too, Margot," she cut the woman off with a snark. "I'm well, thanks for asking."

There was a sigh on the other end of the line. "Rosie. Your proposal is ridiculous."

Having just arrived home, Rosie dropped into her favourite armchair - a big, cushy number which could almost fit two people - and slung one leg over the right arm, bracing her back on the other. Her shoes had been toed off at the door moments earlier, so she was free to wriggle her stocking-clad toes to get the blood flowing properly again. Wearing heels was *the worst.* With her head resting against the cushioned backrest, she frowned. "Why? I mean, come on; you let Nancy write that piece about gum the other day. This has got to be more entertaining than that."

"*I Chew, Chew, Chews You!* was hilarious," Margot defended, ignoring Rosie's scoff, "and substantially more light-hearted than your idea. Less time-consuming to put it together, too."

Though Margot couldn't see her, Rosie pinched the bridge of her nose with her free hand. This was where four years of university had gotten her? A grown-ass woman was debating with her about an article extolling the virtues of chewing gum, for Christ's sake! "It was boring," she countered, "and a ten-year-old could have written it. My suggestion has the appeal of Human Interest."

"Admittedly, it does have that car-crash-can't-look-away-morbid-curiosity feel to it, but it'll take you time to *research*," came the reply. Rosie could imagine her editor using her fingers to form quotation marks as she spat the word 'research' down the line. "You've got to give me something else for this week's deadline."

A smirk slowly crept across Rosie's face. "So, you're saying that once it's written, you'll publish it? As long as I'm still pumping out the drivel in the meantime?"

"It's not *drivel*, Rose."

It was worse, actually. It was click-bait. But she held her tongue and replied, "Sorry. *Quicker, lighter articles.*" Honestly, she could probably tap-dance on her keyboard and nobody would notice as long as people were still clicking on the links and being bombarded by the advertising which kept their company afloat. But there was no joy in that. At least, not for Rosie.

Margot made a sound of vague approval before promptly terminating the call.

"Great. Good chat. Bye to you too," Rosie muttered, putting her phone back in her pocket.

She didn't really know why she was defending her proposal so vehemently, to be honest. It was just a fluff piece (anything their site *ever* published was just fluff) but from the instant the idea had sprouted in her brain she had wanted to do it.

Margot was right: it would take a lot more time to research and collate the data than their usual articles did. That wasn't necessarily a bad thing in Rosie's opinion. She was dying to put her skills as an investigative journalist to the test. And, okay, this wasn't exactly what Rosie initially had in mind when she'd gone off to uni, but it was better than sitting around and writing about the latest viral tweets she'd seen, or what product KMart was currently selling as an absolute 'must have'.

"Whatcha thinkin' so hard about?" Her older brother's voice came out of nowhere, startling her enough to let out a shrill cry of surprise. *At least*, she mused wryly, *I didn't fall off my chair this time.*

She glared at the man who was now bent over at the apartment door in a fit of laughter. "Micah!" she huffed. "What have I told you about just letting yourself in?" Honestly, she'd known giving her brother a key had been a mistake.

Still grinning and completely unrepentant, Micah sauntered into the lounge properly and dropped into the adjacent couch. He casually ran a hand through his chestnut-coloured hair. "I didn't even expect you to be home."

"And that somehow makes it better?!" She was *so* taking her key back.

Micah shrugged. "I had an audition just down the street, and I've got another one in a couple of hours in the city. There's no point going back to my own place."

Rosie shook her head but accepted that this was her own doing. Their mother had basically guilt-tripped her into looking after her big brother, knowing she was the more responsible and mature of the two of them. So, for the time being, she would deal with Micah using her apartment as a home away from home, eating her food and usurping her TV, but would continue to threaten to take away Micah's key just to make herself feel in control.

"So," Micah continued, oblivious to Rosie's musings, "what was all that frowning about when I came in? You know it'll give you wrinkles."

Rosie snorted. Micah's obsession with his own aesthetics was a constant source of amusement to her, despite understanding that, as an actor, it was part of Micah's job to stay pretty. "It was nothing. Just lost in thought."

"You looked pretty serious, kiddo." Blue eyes, which had previously been mirthful, narrowed at her as they took on a more assessing glint. "You weren't thinking about Dumbass again, were you?"

Ah, Dumbass. Conventionally known as Damian, Rosie's ex. "Actually, no, I wasn't."

Micah didn't appear convinced.

Shoulders slumped in resignation, Rosie admitted, "It was actually a work thing."

"Don't you just write crap about whatever's trending?"

"Yep. But I put through a proposal for an article today that's a bit different. I mean, still clickbaity, but...*different*."

Micah chuckled, leaning forward in interest. "Wanna vague that up some more for me?"

"I suggested," and even as she said the words, Rosie knew exactly how her brother would react, "that I write a piece about tracking down all of my crushes over the years, confess the way I'd felt about them and include the reaction from there."

"Rosie..."

"It'd be clickbait *gold*," she forged on, listing reasons on her fingers. "There's the human-interest factor, the drama factor, the embarrassment factor-"

"This is not a good idea." Micah interrupted, shaking his head for emphasis. "Seriously, Rosemary. You can't put yourself out there like that."

Rosie rolled her eyes at her brother's dramatics. "I'm mostly just going to send a couple of Facebook messages," she explained in the same tone one might try with a two-year-old. "I'm not humiliating myself in person."

Micah's lips drew into a thin line. "And what if these guys are married now, or in serious relationships, or if they have kids? You don't think it's a little unfair to send them all a 'Surprise! I had a crush on you!' message and disrupt their lives?" It was almost amusing that this was coming from her perpetually single cad of a brother, but it was a valid point.

"Well obviously I won't contact anyone whose status doesn't say they're single." She had already given this a bit of thought.

"Uh huh. And if they don't have Facebook?"

Rosie shrugged. "Then I'll do more research, won't I? I'm not setting out to ruin anyone's life here, Mike. It's just a spot of fun."

Her brother leaned back, defeated. "I'm just worried about you, kiddo."

"I'm twenty-eight, Micah. Not a kid." Being eight years her elder, she felt like Micah would never lose his infernal nickname for her. She suspected he used it purely to rile her up, too.

As predicted, her protest went ignored, but she was taken aback by the concern in his voice that followed. "It's just..." he waved his hand about as he searched for the right words, "you're opening up a can of worms with this one. I don't think you realise how much this could backfire on you. You're a pretty sensitive person, Rose. I don't want your heart getting broken all over again." The phrase 'like it did with Damian' went unsaid, but she heard it, nonetheless.

It was kind of a sweet sentiment, especially coming from her big brother. Rosie sent him a reassuring smile. "It's just a bit of fun for a fluff article. And I was never in love with these people, I just crushed on them a little. Nobody's going to get hurt, I swear."

* * *

"Son of a...*fucking fuck*," Grant hissed in pain as hot coffee scalded his thighs and stained his trousers.

"Having a good day, then?" Rosie asked playfully, leaning against the partition at his desk. She'd been on her way to the copier when her colleague had cried out.

Grant Sydney was one of the few people she actually got along with in the office. He was tall, dark, sinfully attractive, had a sharp tongue and an even sharper sense of humour, if somewhat crude at times. He had absolutely no filter between his brain and his mouth, was an incorrigible flirt and was always fun to talk to.

He glared at the mug on his desk. "Aside from being betrayed by the one I love most," he responded. "Someone needs to invent spill proof coffee."

"Or you need to pay more attention to what you're doing."

"That's just crazy talk."

Rosie laughed, giving him a fond look. "So, what'd you pitch this week?"

He reached for a wad of tissues and attempted to mop at the mess he had made of his lap and desk. "Ugh," he complained, "I couldn't think of anything, so I basically said I'd write about my favourite TV shows growing up and how they've aged or dated or whatever."

"That's not awful," Rosie shook her head, glad to have her riotous curls tamed into a bun for the day, "It's an excuse to break out the snacks and watch TV, right?"

"Yeah, but it's been done before. It all gets a bit old, don't you think?" Grant had abandoned attempting to salvage the splodge on his thigh, sat back in his chair and met her gaze. "What'd you come up with?"

Given that both Micah and Margot had both poo-pooed the idea, Rosie was hesitant to tell her friend lest she had to defend her concept again. "Well, I pitched an idea which might take some time to come together, but this week I'll be writing about the surprising uses of shaving cream," she completed her sentence with jazz hands. "For cleaning and such."

His dark brown eyes seemed to shine with mirth, "Shaving cream, huh? Not whipped cream?"

"Maybe I'll save that one for another day."

He grinned at her, completely unrepentant. "So, tell me about this longer project. I wasn't aware this was the kind of site that published anything serious."

"It's not serious," she was quick to refute, "just a touch long-winded in the prep work."

Grant's grin turned into a predatory smirk. Jabbing a pen in her direction, he accused, "You're being cagey, Rosemary Weiss. You're not great at being sneaky so you might as well tell your good friend Grant what you're tiptoeing around."

"You'll laugh at me," she protested through another laugh of her own, clutching her forgotten photocopying to her chest.

"And that's different to every other day how?"

He made a good point, she supposed. They did tend to bicker and tease each other about practically everything, almost like siblings. "I don't know," she hedged, "I guess because the topic is kind of personal."

"Honey," he soothed, but there was a playful expression on his face which didn't bode well for her, "Nancy has already done a comparison on menstrual cups, remember?"

Rosie hit his bicep with her folder of paperwork, "You're such a dick."

"You know you love me."

"Hmm," she mused dismissively. "No, I'm not going to be writing about my damn period, but thanks for proving you've still got the maturity of a thirteen-year-old."

"Hey!" Grant chuckled. "You told me it was 'personal' and that's girl code, isn't it?"

"You're an idiot."

He raised his hands in mock surrender. "Guilty as charged. Now tell me this grand idea of yours."

Feeling self-conscious, she fiddled with the corner of the folder in her arms. "Essentially, I'm going to send a few Facebook messages to some of my past crushes and then document their responses."

There was a beat of silence before Grant started to laugh: a booming, infectious sound which had most of their office peering around partitions with curiosity. She sighed and muttered an "I told you so," under her breath.

"*That…*" he started, forcing himself to calm, "Rosie, that's all sorts of fucked up. But I like it."

Well, she thought, *that's the best response so far.*

"I just thought it would bring more traffic in," she responded with a nod to his opinion. "I mean, who doesn't love reading about someone else's relationship trainwrecks?"

He shook his head, his dark hair falling into his eyes. "You've got balls, Weiss, I'll give you that."

She grinned.

Grant leaned back in his chair again, his hands behind his head. "So, what's the plan of attack, then? Are you going to do a follow up article if some of the responses are positive? Like 'What's It Like To Hook Up With A Past Crush' or some shit?"

Rosie made a face. "Ugh, no. I'm not really planning on seeing any of these people in person. That'd be too much, even for crazy old me." No, she was much braver from behind a computer screen and a keyboard, bolstered by wine. "I'm just going to cyber stalk them, send off a few messages to the ones who are still single because I'm not going for the homewrecker vibe-"

She ignored the 'cough "this time" cough' which interrupted her. Honestly, that had been *one date*, and it had been an accident. The wanker had told her he was single. Instead, she rolled her eyes and continued to speak as though he hadn't cut her off. "-and I'll publish the responses along with a write up about my anxiety about sending the messages and how it all panned out for me."

Grant was eyeing her speculatively. "It might all backfire, you realise."

"Well, now you sound like my brother."

He perked up, sitting up straighter, eyes gleaming with renewed interest. "The super hot one?"

She huffed good-naturedly, "I only have the one brother."

"Yeah, I just like acknowledging how attractive he is." Grant's smirk was definitely predatory now.

Shaking her head and with an amused smile, she pushed off from the partition she'd been relaxing against. "And he loves having it acknowledged. You're just feeding his ego."

"He's not even here!" Grant called after Rosie as she made her way back down the hallway, finally remembering her photocopying.

Over her shoulder, she shot back, "And, oh look! Neither am I."

* * *

Going home to a silent, empty apartment was absolute bliss. It was only a shoebox, but it was perfect for her needs. Rosie had a bedroom, tiny ensuite, and an open plan combined living and kitchen area. A cupboard by the front door served as her laundry. With her apartment situated on the fourth floor of the complex, it even had a snippet of a view of the city.

Kicking her shoes off at the door, she leaned against the cool timber for a moment, relishing in her private sanctuary. Her mother was convinced that living on her own was a mistake. "You'll be lonely," she'd said, worrying her hands together. "And it's not safe. And I'll never see you." Sometimes, Rosie even suspected Micah was over as often as he was just to appease their mother's nagging.

But it was her idea of heaven. There was nobody to distract her from her writing, or to switch stations on the TV, or to whine about her music choices.

She could languish in her bathtub for hours on end or stay in bed longer on a weekend without feeling the pressure to get up and socialise. And if she wanted to get takeaway three nights in a row, there was nobody to judge her.

Even in that moment, as she padded around the living room and into her tiny kitchen, she took advantage of her solitude, removing her bra with a sigh of relief as she went. She grabbed her favourite (read: largest) wine glass and a half-empty bottle of her favourite red wine and happily dropped down onto the welcoming comfort of her couch. A couple of quick flicks of her Harry Potter Wand TV Remote (she had no regrets with that purchase) and she was lost in the land of Netflix.

Rosie had finished her wine and three episodes of *Nailed It!* when she decided she had procrastinated enough. After selecting a new bottle of wine and cracking it open, she switched the TV off and gave herself a rousing shake.

"Alrighty, let's do this thing," she said to herself, retrieving her laptop from the coffee table. Facebook loaded up and her cursor hovered over the search bar.

"I guess we'll go chronologically," she decided before typing the name of her first real adolescent crush. Matthew Saville. Year Six. All the other girls had been just as into him, and hadn't he known it? *Smug little shit*, she mused, sipping at her wine.

At this point, she was simply doing reconnaissance. Seeing if she could even find half these people would be the first step. The next step: double checking that they weren't in serious relationships. The final step would be to send messages.

Initially, she had toyed with the idea of telling her test subjects that she was doing research on their reactions, but then realised doing so might lead them to provide responses which could potentially be rehearsed or disingenuous.

Rosie's eyes scanned the list of results, looking for a hint of a familiar face. This was actually proving more difficult than she had thought it would because there were so many results and half of them had profile pictures which gave no clue as to what the account owners even looked like. And there were none who shared any mutual friends with her (not a surprise -

her friend list was fairly short) so she'd reached a dead end there. "Think, think, think," she told herself. "Who was Matthew friends with? Or is he going by Matt or Matty instead of Matthew?"

With some more time and even more wine, she finally found him. She hoped.

The man in the profile photo looked kind of like the boy she'd known in primary school, except for a distinct lack of hair. She clicked on his profile, feeling a little like a creeper for doing so, and was unsurprised to find it set to private mode, with very little information or photos available.

Her heart hammered in her chest as she contemplated sending him a private message. What was she supposed to say? 'Hey, remember me from Grade Six? Just wondering if you're in a relationship.' That wasn't exactly smooth or subtle. She was supposed to be an investigative journalist - surely a little Facebook stalking wasn't going to break her on the first attempt.

Setting this one aside for now, she moved onto Crush Number Two: James Crockford. Grade Eight. He'd been a really sweet kid, with brown eyes and a smattering of freckles over his nose and cheeks. She'd liked him because he'd always been friendly to her, never joining in on any of the bitching or teasing she had suffered from other kids for being a bit chubby in her adolescence. As she'd aged, her curves had only become more emphasised, and she was comfortable and confident in her skin. But the schoolyard taunts had hurt at the time, and anyone not participating in the bullying had been someone to cling to, whether they were aware of it or not.

James was easier to find. However, his profile picture displayed him with two small children and his relationship status read that he was married.

"Next!" she declared, pouring herself another generous glass of cabernet sauvignon.

Number Three. She crinkled her nose at this one. Stefan Grace. Grade Ten and a total cliche. Tall, handsome, popular, star athlete… *Ugh*. What the hell had she been thinking? She couldn't recall speaking to him much at all outside of English class, and yet she had been besotted.

Facebook led her to him fairly easily too, and she almost swallowed her own tongue at his profile picture. "Oh my God." He'd grown up in all the best ways if his shirtless picture was anything to go by. His Relationship Status was listed as 'Single'. Rose's lips curled into a smirk. "Bingo."

Fortified by a full bottle of red wine, she clicked the 'send message' icon and began to type.

Chapter Two

Somewhere in the middle of a dream starring an actor Rosie harboured a crush on (a man with a chiselled jaw and dark eyes which made her a little weak-kneed, and that was to say nothing of his deep voice and boyish grin) an irritating sound rent the air. Ringing. Ongoing ringing.

Her dream companion frowned, "Aren't you gonna answer that?"

"What?" she asked him, already feeling the tropical island atmosphere around them warping and disappearing. The ringing continued. She clung desperately to the edges of her dream.

"Answer your damn phone." Those words roused her, coming from somewhere firmly rooted in reality. She groaned piteously as she woke up on her couch.

Her brother was frowning at her from the armchair.

With a mouth which felt like something furry had died in it, Rosie asked, "Micah?" Her head throbbed at the effort. "Ugh, I feel like I've been hit by a truck."

"A couple of bottles of red will do that to you." Her brother's reply was dispassionate as he gestured to the empty bottles he'd found on the coffee table in front of them.

"One was practically empty when I started it," she defended, shutting her eyes. "I've gotta get a chain lock installed on that door."

When she finally picked up her phone there was a Facebook message waiting for her, as well as three missed calls from Margot and a curt text message from her demanding an immediate call back. Against Rosie's better judgement, she went straight to the Facebook message.

"What the...?" she asked rhetorically, barely recognising the name or profile picture of the sender.

From the armchair, Micah leaned forward, trying - and failing - to get a glimpse of her phone screen. "What?" he asked, craning his neck.

With her brows furrowed, Rosie tried to make sense of what she was seeing. To start with, she did not remember writing the message she had apparently sent and cringed as she took in the things she had written. She was *so* never drinking and working again! Ignoring the typos and the grammatical issues, the message screamed 'drunken ex'; she wanted the ground to just open up and swallow her whole. "Oh no," she muttered, feeling her cheeks grow warm. "No, no, no, no, no."

Jimmy. She'd messaged Jimmy. Her first 'official' (in a time before Facebook) boyfriend. She'd been sixteen.

Her face must have shown her dawning horror because Micah's hand was now on her forearm, forcing her to look up at him. "What's wrong?" he asked, with concern. None of his prior apathy or amusement was present. "Rose?"

"I did something very, very stupid." Her heart was hammering hard in her chest, nausea beginning to swirl in her belly. She dragged a hand down her face. "Oh God, I am never, ever drinking again. Ever."

"Okay, okay, calm down." It wasn't often Micah went into 'big brother' mode, but she was glad he was doing so now instead of relying on a good old fashioned 'I told you so'. He moved to sit beside her on the couch, wrapping an arm around her shoulders. "What did you do?"

Swallowing thickly, Rosie shut her eyes and rested her head on his shoulder. "Do you remember the summer after Grade Ten? *My* Grade Ten, obviously."

"Vaguely," he replied cautiously. "What does that have to do with..." he trailed off, glancing at Rosie's phone, then the two empty bottles of wine, then the laptop lying discarded on the coffee table. Next, clearly recalling their conversation about her planned project, he released an explosive sigh.

13

"Who did you message?"

"Did you ever meet Jimmy?" she asked by way of reply, assaulted by memories of that summer. They'd met while she'd been working at the local cinema. It had taken him returning to the cinema daily for the better part of a week for her to realise that he was genuinely interested in her and not asking her out as part of some elaborate hoax. He'd been tall and kind of gangly, and she'd preened under his attention, not used to boys ever actually noticing her.

Micah shrugged. "It was a long time ago and I had my own stuff going on. Keeping up with my kid sister's social life wasn't big on my list of priorities."

"Point," she acknowledged, deciding to just bite the bullet. "Well, Jimmy was my first boyfriend."

Sitting up again now, she watched as her brother's lips curled upwards into a smirk. "Really?" he asked, drawing out the word and sounding a little like a Bond villain. She smacked at his arm.

"It wasn't like *that*. I mean, I know he wanted it to be, but I was sixteen and insecure, so..." she shook her head. "There was a *lot* of making out, though." Rosie couldn't help the wistful tone which crept into her voice with the admission.

Micah's blue eyes shone with mirth. "Alright, so, first boyfriend. It's him you messaged?"

Wincing, she bobbed her head, her dark curls, knotted from her sleep on the couch, shifting into her face. Rosie brushed her errant locks back behind her ears with her fingers. "Unfortunately." She did not want to think about the words she'd written, and she hadn't yet read his reply. Mortified, she considered changing her name and moving to another country. "He probably thinks I'm a lunatic."

"Can I read it?" Micah was reaching for her phone, but she hastily shoved it aside, vehemently refusing.

"This is humiliating enough," she justified when her brother rolled his eyes at her. The words were burned inside her brain with phrases like 'I've been thinking of you' and 'you should have been my first' making her squirm and want to vomit.

14

Rosie had no idea where they'd come from. She hadn't thought about Jimmy in years. However, there was nothing she could do to take them back or fix this stupid mistake. She couldn't bring herself to read his reply, for fear that it could potentially cement her utter mortification and send her hurtling back to a time where she'd been vulnerable and so very unsure of herself. How had she gone from sending a simple message to a crush to chasing down her first boyfriend and making a fool of herself?

"I'm sure it's not that bad," Micah tried again, his tone soft and placating. "Whatever you sent him, I'm sure he was probably even flattered that, twelve years on, you're still thinking about him."

Rosie groaned. "I sound like a stalker." Seriously, her heart was hammering heavily in her chest. She did not want to face the world right then. "Especially because the way I broke up with him wasn't stellar."

"Hang on. *You* broke up with *him*?"

She didn't love the incredulity in the way he asked the question, emphasizing 'you' and 'him' with disbelief. "Is that so surprising?"

"No, of course not." With his squared jaw, chiselled cheek bones and flopsy brown hair, Micah was very used to schooling his expression into a believably angelic moue of contrition. But he was an actor and she had known him her whole life, so this didn't fool her.

Taking a calming breath, Rosie waved her hand dismissively. 'Whatever," she said, understanding his perspective perfectly well. "It doesn't matter."

He didn't appear entirely convinced, but he asked, "So what makes the breakup so awkward, then? Because you were teenagers, so I can't imagine it was anything too crazy. It's not like he caught you in bed with his sister or anything."

Blinking at him, she decided she did not need to know how or why that was the first example he conjured up. Instead, Rosie bit her lip before confessing, "I told him the truth."

"The truth?"

And, yeah, putting it that way made it sound benign, but Rosie knew better. "Mum wanted me to break up with him. It was a bit of a trainwreck, actually." During the entire course of their relationship, Jimmy had been really sweet,

15

but dumping him in public, accidentally in front of his friends at that, had flipped a switch. He'd called her a coward and said some other stuff which was probably warranted, all things considered. It had still stung, though. "I felt awful about it for years."

A few seconds of silence passed before Micah snorted. "That's it?"

"What?"

"Is that it?" he repeated, as if the painful, embarrassing moment of her life which she had just shared was inadequately awkward.

She wasn't going any further into detail with him, though. "Yeah, I guess."

He frowned; she could read his reproach without him having to say the words. Rosie could see the '*I call bullshit*' clear as day on her brother's face. But she figured Micah also knew there would likely be a bigger, scarier trainwreck that could possibly arise from this than this moment of embarrassment, so it seemed to her that he opted to save his energy. "Alright, I have to bounce anyway."

She was used to her brother being dismissive and flighty. Sometimes it bothered her. At other times, such as that moment, it was a Godsend.

Once he was gone and it was safe to look, she peered down at the message.

Jimmy's response was short, but not the mocking or the rejection she had anticipated. Instead, the words which met her read: '*Can we talk about this over drinks?*'

Drinks? What did *drinks* mean? A date? That was very likely what he'd meant, given that the things she had written to him were far from platonic.

Her first instinct was a resounding 'no'. *But, then again,* she mused with her thumbs hovering over her phone screen, *why not?*

She clicked on his profile and a small smile tugged at the corner of her lips when she viewed the larger version of his profile picture: a close up of his face, his hazel eyes blown wide as he beamed at the camera. He looked the same as he had when they were teenagers, just older. His profile said he was single (thank goodness) and it didn't look like he posted very often.

Despite her earlier mortification, she slid the notification to the side and typed her reply, curiosity winning out over caution and embarrassment. '*Sure. When & where?*' She pressed send before she could change her mind.

To distract herself, she called Margot back immediately following this. Her boss answered on the second ring. "Where the hell are you?"

"I'm running really late. I'm sorry. I'll work late tonight."

There was a huff of impatience from the other end of the call. "Not what I asked, Rose."

"I'm at home. I overslept." There was no sense lying to the woman, and it wasn't as if their office was a conventional one. They ran a website for crying out loud! Rosie had no idea why they needed an office at all - all the work could be completed from literally anywhere in the world. "I'm really sorry, Margot."

A beat. "You're lucky you're one of my most popular writers, you know."

Rosie got up off the couch and made her way into her bedroom, balancing her phone between her ear and shoulder while she shimmied out of her pjs and hopped around on one leg, attempting to get into her dark wash denim jeans. "Yeah, I know, and again, I'm sorry."

"At least you met deadline. Nancy missed hers, which is why I need you here ASAP. We'll need some filler for tomorrow."

With a stash of click-bait ideas up her sleeve, Rosie nodded despite her boss not being able to see her. "Got it," she acknowledged, "I'll be there in twenty."

"See me as soon as you get in," Margot demanded, terminating the call.

* * *

Rosie received a reply from Jimmy just as she stepped into the elevator that would take her up to the office.

'Free tonight?' it read.

She stared at it, unsure that she'd read it correctly, and almost missed her floor as a result.

"Earth to Rosemary," Grant's voice roused her from her stupor, which enabled her to step out of the elevator just before the doors closed on her; she quietly apologised to the disgruntled passengers she left behind.

Grant was leaning against the wall in the hallway, two takeaway coffees in hand. He passed her one, which she gratefully accepted. "Figured you'd need this," he told her.

"God yes," she enthused, savouring the aroma before taking her first sip. She made an obscene sound of approval. "My hero." Grant beamed at her, and she shook her head, "I was talking to the coffee."

"Someone's in a mood," he observed, falling into step with her while she headed towards Margot's office.

She shot him a look of disdain, then, remembering the coffee he'd gifted her with, softened her expression and on a sigh admitted, "I've had a shitty morning."

Margot was tapping a pen against her glass desk, appearing to be deep in concentration when the pair entered her office. She changed her focus and shot out a quick group message and assembled the rest of the writers to her office. Nancy was glaringly absent. "Let's go around the room," Margot demanded without preamble.

Rosie hated every minute of it. How was this her job? Who actually read this shit? Seriously.

After the meeting, they shuffled out of Margot's office and walked back to their workspaces. Rosie pulled up the Notes app on her phone and started typing nonsense into it about lint. She was half done (after a total of four minutes) when Grant swung in to interrupt her, rapping on the side of her cubicle with the back of his knuckles.

"Hard at work or hardly working?"

Setting her phone screen side down on her desk, Rosie rolled her eyes and sat back in her chair, peering up at her colleague with a sense of nonchalance that she didn't quite feel. "My dad says that, just so you're aware of the calibre of your jokes today."

"I don't know; your dad sounds like a pretty cool guy."

The look she gave him in return was a flat one. "He wears Crocs," she paused for effect, "with socks."

Shuddering, Grant dipped his head. "Okay, point taken."

"So, did you want something?"

"What? I can't just stop by my good friend Rosemary's desk for a chat?"

He did a pretty good job at feigning innocence, but she knew him well.

"No," Rosie informed him.

Grant laughed, his dark eyes practically twinkling with his mirth. "Harsh, Rose."

She drummed her fingers on her desk, unmoved by the sentiment of his words. "Come on," she prodded, "Out with it. Some of us are actually trying to work."

"Like your *literal* fluff piece is going to take you more than ten minutes." The shake of his head accompanying this was indulgent. "Lint? Really?"

Rosie shrugged, gesturing to her blouse. "I was inspired," she drawled, earning herself another chuckle.

"I see."

Raising both her eyebrows expectantly, Rosie stared up at him.

"Okay, fine. Your brother, the hot one-"

"The only one."

"The hot one," Grant nodded, completely ignoring her interruption, "sent me a Facebook message. I was super excited, until I realised the topic of conversation was you and not his overwhelming desire to take me to dinner."

"You really know how to make a girl feel loved," she snarked, before realising what he'd said. "Hang on, *what?*" She sat bolt upright, extending her hand in askance for his phone. "He did what?"

Grant took a step backwards out of her reach, sliding his phone from his pocket. "He's very sweet," he assured her, but the words did little to soothe her annoyance, "and says you were upset this morning because, and I quote, 'She drunk messaged an ex-boyfriend with something embarrassing and had a meltdown. Can you make sure she's okay?' which makes him even more of a catch, you realise."

Her jaw dropped and she blinked while she processed this new onslaught of humiliation. "I'm going to kill him."

"Not until after you've given me all the details," he chided, inviting himself into her cubicle and sitting on the corner of her desk, disrupting a notebook and scattering her highlighters in the process. "Can't have you hauled off to prison until after I've been entertained, can we?"

19

"So, at this point that's a real possibility."

Grant raised his eyebrows, still blatantly amused. "Which part? The prison or the entertainment?"

"Who's to say the two have to be mutually exclusive?" Rosie bantered back, before shaking her head. "But I meant prison. Micah's dead to me."

Her colleague made a 'tsk'ing sound as he picked up one of her pens and twirled it about between his fingers. "He cares about you. It's very sweet."

"Dead. To. Me."

Grant's wide smile told her he didn't believe her for a second. He jutted the pen in her direction. "So, what's going on?"

It took her about ten seconds to get him up to speed. At the end of her story, he frowned. "In all seriousness, Rose, you're gonna be careful with this, right?"

"Of course," she responded dutifully, barely refraining from rolling her eyes. Did nobody think she was mature enough to handle this? Her thoughts skidded to the messages she'd exchanged with Jimmy and she winced mentally. Okay, so as long as she avoided the vino, she'd be able to handle it. "I've got this."

Grant seemed to come to the same conclusion because he abandoned the pen he'd been fiddling with and reached for his phone again. "This message says otherwise."

She huffed at him as his comment reminded her of why she wanted to cheerfully strangle her brother. "Well, I've got a date out of it."

Grant grew even more sceptical. "There are a million murder documentaries on Netflix outlining why going on that date sounds like a bad idea."

"You're being ridiculous," Rosie told him, pushing him off her desk and setting her notes and stationery back to rights. "If Micah hadn't messaged you, you'd be asking all sorts of inappropriate questions which would likely get you fired."

Grant's eyebrows drew together. "In all the years we've worked together, I've never known you to get drunk and text an ex. It's out of character for you, and so I'm just a tad concerned."

The seriousness of the conversation made her uncomfortable. Grant was her playful, flirty friend. If anyone was acting out of character, it was him. Rosie shifted in her seat and offered him her best smile. "I'm fine. Really. And you're not changing my mind on this."

He stared her down, his eyes flickering between hers as though weighing the conviction of her words. Eventually, he seemed to give up. "Ugh. Fine." He walked away frowning.

Rosie's gaze drifted to her phone, to the unanswered message she'd been ignoring.

Knowing she would pay hell for it later, she shot a text to Margot saying something had come up, scooped up her handbag and headed for the door.

* * *

"I've got to stop falling asleep on this couch," Rosie lamented when her alarm went off. She had a perfectly good bed, one which had cost her an arm and a leg because she'd splurged on a 'good' mattress, literally a few steps away. Drinks with Jimmy (the first test subject for her article) had been an unmitigated disaster culminating in him throwing a drink in her face, and her dragging herself home in defeat.

She was still delightfully alone, no irritating big brother making his presence known and no phone calls from her boss demanding her attention. She stretched and yawned in a fair impression of a large, pyjama-clad cat. Forcing herself up, she made a coffee and eyed the breakfast cereal on the shelf, wondering if it was worth the effort. Her stomach rumbled so she gave in, deciding that a fed Rosie was less likely to be a cranky Rosie.

She wound up wolfing down her breakfast and then dressed for the day, managing to wrangle her unruly curls into a bun at the nape of her neck before she snapped up her handbag, slid her feet into her favourite flats and made her way out of her apartment.

The sky outside was overcast, the air heavy and humid. Belatedly, she thought she probably should have grabbed an umbrella, but she couldn't be bothered heading back up to her place to go find one. Pulling her phone from her handbag, she registered that there was a text from her brother but nothing from anyone else and she slumped a little in disappointment. Ignoring Micah for the time being, she brought up her Uber app, arranged a ride to work, and then procrastinated with calling her brother a while longer by flipping through her Facebook feed.

Her Uber pulled up and inspiration struck her. The fluff piece of the day would be 'How to Keep Your 5 Star Uber Passenger Rating'. Yes, it had been done before, but she couldn't care less. Margot would eat it up, especially with Rosie's additional flair for being a bit biting and exaggerated with her humour.

By the time the car came to a stop outside the office, she was finished writing the bones of the article. She thanked the driver and made her way through the glass doors into the foyer of the building. Her ballet flats slapped against the glossy tiled floors as she crossed the space to the bank of three elevators. She pressed the 'up' button and, when the middle elevator's doors swung open, hopped in, wondering how she would occupy the next eight hours considering her work was already done. Working on her human-interest project, which was quickly becoming more so a selfish activity, perchance?

The entire exercise chasing up old crushes and boyfriends was obviously being fuelled by some sort of inherent desire to find acceptance and love and settle down, as much as she wanted to think otherwise. A fight against the innate dissatisfaction at the way her life had turned out or something along those lines.

She stifled a frustrated scream. No, this was just a spot of fun. *Fun, fun, fun*. If she repeated the mantra enough, she might just believe it.

Eventually, she made her way to her cubicle and replied to the text from her brother.

'*How'd the date go?*' his text asked. Rosie imagined him saying it teasingly because that was just who he was.

Her expression twisted, recalling the humiliation all too easily. '*Not great.*'

It took less than ten seconds for Micah to reply. '*Are you okay?*'

The question surprised her, but then again, it wasn't a far stretch of the imagination that her brother for all his cad-like behaviour was actually a softie at heart.

She smiled despite herself. *'Yeah,'* she typed out, *'I'm fine.'*

It took a couple more minutes for his reply to come through. *'Here if you need anything. I'll see you at Dad's thing. I might have some news to share. Might not. We'll see. Either way, I'm a bit tied up right now.'*

Rosie frowned. The event scheduled for their father's birthday wasn't for another two days. Two days without her no-boundaries brother wasn't normal. He was keeping his distance. She couldn't help but be suspicious. What was he hiding? Maybe unravelling this mystery would distract her from her sudden need to seek out a relationship. She could only hope.

'What?' she typed, adding a little shocked face emoji. *'You're not going to be usurping my couch and eating my food for the next couple of days? You feeling okay?'*

'Ha ha.' Was the only reply she received.

Well, there goes that plan. She sighed. It seemed that whatever was going on with her wayward sibling would not be resolved via text message.

Despite wanting to distract herself, Rosie pulled up a Word document on her computer and jotted down some notes about her failed date with Jimmy and their history. At least she knew she could spin it into something witty and hilarious with the right degree of exaggeration, which made the entire encounter a little easier to stomach.

She made sure to note that throwing a drink in one's face, though mildly abusive, was never an acceptable way to attack anyone just because one might be *feeling things*. But nothing outside of her ego had been hurt, and humour was her coping mechanism. Plugging in her headphones and pressing the play button on an upbeat playlist, she typed and edited her work down to a few paragraphs which actually amused her.

When work was over, she slung her handbag over her shoulder and jumped in the elevator. Part of her was marginally disappointed that she hadn't been accosted by Grant at all over the course of the day, but he had his own shit to do, and they often went days without contact, particularly with deadlines looming over their heads.

Out on the street, the sky had broken open. Rain was pouring down.

Rosie ordered another Uber home and loitered under the shelter of the front of the building until the promised car came to a stop. She used her handbag as a makeshift umbrella (it was a fifteen-dollar knockoff and she had a whole collection at home should this one become ruined) and dashed to the passenger seat, politely greeting the driver and sharing that awkward small-talk moment of lamenting over the weather.

The drive home was short. Rosie thanked her driver again and then dashed to the shelter of her apartment block. She still managed to look like a drowned rat by the time she made it inside. "Guess that's twice in a row," she muttered to herself.

"They say talking to yourself is the first sign of insanity," the neighbour from the unit directly below hers - Jason? Jackson? Jameson? She could never remember his name! - joked as he came up beside her while she checked the mail.

She hoped the smile she gave him was pleasant and not as forced as it felt. "So, is answering myself the second one?"

He laughed while she flicked through the stack of envelopes in her hand. Junk, junk, coupon, junk, bill, junk...invitation? She hazarded a guess on the last one, interested enough that she opened it while she maintained half a bland conversation with the creepy neighbour.

It was an invitation to an old friend's wedding, though technically Brennan was more Micah's friend than her own. She smothered a sigh. *Great.*

Johnson? (no, that was too far-fetched) peered over her shoulder. "Ugh," he groaned in commiseration, "aren't those the worst? Having to find a date and pretend you're super happy for the couple, even though you'll probably be trading bets with other guests on how long they'll last."

Rosie couldn't quite school her face beyond the arched eyebrow of judgement. This guy knew nothing of Brennan and Jeff, the newly engaged couple, and had no idea that her resistance had nothing to do with the party and everything to do with how lame her own love life was.

All in all, she really didn't appreciate this guy's snooping. "Speak for yourself," she told him, slipping the coupon, bill and invitation into her sodden handbag, tossing the junk mail into the recycling bin kept by the mailboxes specifically for this purpose as she headed for the stairs, "I'm sure it'll be a fun night."

The invitation also seemed to be issued with surprisingly short notice. She only had a week to return her RSVP, with the wedding date looming just over a month away. She couldn't help but glare at the little 'plus one' box that seemed to tease her because she had no reason to check the box suggesting she had a date to bring.

"Need a date?" 'J' called out after her.

She pretended not to hear him.

* * *

The next day, once again seated in her cubicle at work, Rosie pulled out the invitation to Brennan and Jeff's wedding from her handbag, having completely forgotten about it the previous evening. She set it on her desk and sighed. Did she even want to go? Her creepy neighbour had been kind of right: going to these things was usually a drag, unless you were particularly close with the couple or had a group of friends to enjoy the evening with. While it might be nice to celebrate with Brennan, she felt as though having to procure a date and pretend to love her life was going to be too much effort in her current mood.

"What's that?" Grant asked, peering over her shoulder, quite happily inviting himself into her cubicle.

"What? My personal space or the stuff inside it?"

He leaned over her, and she didn't lean closer to him and breathe in the scent of whatever expensive cologne he was wearing. She *didn't*! Okay, she did, but only because he always splurged on the good stuff, smelling insanely sexy, and she had to get her kicks *somewhere*! During her momentary distraction, he plucked the invitation right off her desk.

"This sounds fun," he said, grinning at her indignant squawking. "Are you going to take your date? The one from the other night?"

"I was actually about to politely decline the invitation through the age-old art of text message and avoidance." Her response was delivered primly as she extended her hand, palm facing up. "So, give it back."

He held it out of reach, dark eyes glinting with mirth. "Come now, Rosemary, use your manners."

"I'm not in the mood," she shot back, sulking in her chair. She waved him away. "Keep the damn thing, I don't care."

"Well, that takes all the fun out of it," Grant informed her, dropping the card back down where he'd found it. His tone softened, "You okay?"

"I'm *fine*."

"Uh huh. I've dated enough people to know that when you say those words in *that* tone it actually means someone's death is imminent. Usually my own." He leaned against the corner of her desk, crossing his long legs at the ankles. "So, tell me the truth."

"I'm just in a bit of a rut," she confessed, surprising herself with how easily the words left her mouth. "I'm not feeling inspired by anything right now. And I can't even tell you why. It's not like my life sucks or anything."

He nodded with obvious empathy. "Maybe you just need a break? When was the last time you took a holiday?"

"I...don't even remember. Huh." This revelation was actually a little disturbing.

Grant's expression turned a little wry. "You realise burnout is a thing, right?"

"Yes," she acknowledged with exaggerated patience, "but I'm not feeling burnt out. Just..." she shrugged.

"Unhappy? Unfulfilled? Frustrated?"

Sighing, Rosie nodded, "A little from all three columns."

"Take a holiday," he insisted.

"By myself?" she asked, having never considered doing so before. Was that even a *thing*? "What would I even do?"

"I don't know," Grant responded, pushing himself off her desk and squeezing her shoulders, "Whatever you want. Lie on a beach with a cocktail in hand. Go skiing. Visit Disneyland. Go trekking in Nepal. Who cares what you do as long as it resets your system?" As though he had decided to be sage and dramatic, he left these as his final words before he disappeared towards

26

his own cubicle.

The idea kept rattling in Rosie's head as the day went on. A holiday. It was a surprisingly tantalising concept. Would it get her out of her funk? Part of her thought Grant might be right - it was probably worth a shot to try it. She couldn't even recall the last time she'd been on a holiday. There had been a few long weekend getaways taken with Damian back when they'd been dating, but she couldn't actually recall taking a proper vacation as an adult. That realisation stopped her in her tracks.

Was she really that much of a workaholic?

This thought was somewhat depressing and yet inadvertently she proved her own point by putting her head down and focusing on work as a means to distract herself from her suddenly bleak view of reality. With her brother unexpectedly off the grid (and this was still very suspicious) and Grant giving her space, Rosie's fingers flew across her keyboard without stalling. She pumped out seven more fluff pieces for the website about everything from sugary drinks to sugar daddies and hit 'send all' to Margot.

She had cleared the next week of its deadlines. This meant she didn't have to step foot in the office for several days unless she desperately wanted to, or unless called upon, which was far more likely. Still, she sent an application to Human Resources to use some of her leave hours and clocked off.

For at least a week, the world was her oyster. Rosie had the vague impulse to message another old crush, but she stopped short of creating any more drama for a while. The one-two punch she received from her evening with Jimmy was enough to put her off her endeavours for a little while. There was no specific deadline for that project, so she resolved to look after herself for a little while, or at least make some smarter choices.

However, she still craved some sort of social activity and a friendly ear to discuss her latest issues with. Grant was a fun friend, but she found herself picking up her phone and pulling up her friend Olivia's number.

'Hey Liv,' she texted, glad they had the sort of friendship that could see them not talk for weeks on end (sometimes even months) and then pick up as though it had been a handful of days, *'Outside of Dad's birthday thing, I've got the next few days and weekend free. Thinking a catch up. You in? I can supply wine and cheese.'*

'*When and where?*' was the immediate answer, which made Rosie grin, her thumbs flying over the keyboard.

Chapter Three

"Okay, so the clause on page fifty-three needs to be reworked, otherwise we're at a stalemate," Rob Owens drawled before he leaned back in his leather chair and rolled his eyes, glad that this meeting was purely over the phone. He had it on speaker and swivelled his chair around to face the coastal view behind his desk. He wished more than anything to be out there enjoying nature rather than stuck inside, in a suit, feeling like a corporate monkey.

But he was the boss, and if he didn't show up and work hard how could he expect any of his staff do the same?

The voice on the other end sighed. "If we could see to it that a delay of more than three days isn't penalised quite so heavily-"

"That's not exactly fair on my client, though, is it, Dave?" Rob felt as though he and the other lawyer had been going back and forth over this contract for months. In reality, it had been a few weeks at worst. "For every day the product is late my client is losing money. If your guys can't deliver and are that worried that it'll be a recurring issue, maybe I need to advise Mister Collingworth to break negotiations and find a different vendor."

"Oh, *come on*, Owens..."

Outside the window, Rob watched a small flock of seagulls descend on a group picnicking on the grassy stretch of park which separated the road from the sandy dunes of the beach. A gentle breeze rocked the leaves of the Norfolk Pines which lined the esplanade proper. It was a stunning day and it was taunting him.

"No." Swivelling his chair back around to his desk, he reached for his pen and notepad, despite a laptop sitting open within his reach. He tapped the pen against the paper with mounting irritation. "The terms are more than fair. Your clients are being greedy, Dave, and you and I both know it. Pretty sure they know it, too. Which would be all well and good, but they don't have a monopoly in the industry and-"

"Fine!"

He smirked at the interruption, and the frustrated tone with which it was delivered. Sitting back again in his seat, he gentled his approach again. "Good. So, we rework the clause as previously discussed, and then they'll sign?"

There was a moment of silence, but Rob waited it out. He grinned and pumped his fist into the air when the other lawyer sighed again. "Yeah." There was a brief, chagrined pause. "Yeah, you've got a deal."

"I'm going to need that in writing, Dave."

The other man's chuckle was somewhere between bitterness and amusement. "You're a piece of work, Owens," he said, but Rob could hear the smile in his voice. They'd worked together a number of times over the years, and he knew just how far he could push the other lawyer. "I'm sending the email now."

"Good man," Rob leaned across the polished timber of his desk, his index finger hovering over the button that would terminate the call. "Have a good week, mate. I'll get the new contract through to you ASAP."

The call ended and he brought up the document (pre-prepared, because he'd known he would win) on his laptop screen, then attached it to his reply to Dave's promised email. "Another one down," he muttered to himself, before closing the lid of the computer and grabbing his keys. He couldn't bear sitting in his office for a minute longer. It was time for a late lunch.

* * *

"How are you still single?" Rob's mate, Pete, asked sarcastically from across the pub table, shaking his head at the mess Rob had made with his burger.

"Not my fault," the lawyer argued, his jacket and tie discarded over the back of the seat next to him. He wiped at his mouth with a napkin, and glanced down at his white shirt, amazed that it had survived the meal unscathed. "The structural integrity of the bun didn't hold."

Pete laughed. "Always got an answer, don't you?"

"It's gotten your sorry arse out of a jam or two, hasn't it?" Rob grinned back.

He'd made the right call leaving the office for the afternoon. He loved his job and, when he had started his own practice, he had known that the hours would be long and that the work would be tedious, but he was beginning to feel restless within his own skin. Catching up with an old friend was enough to tide him over and have him feeling more like himself again.

"I didn't say it was a bad thing, did I?" Pete pilfered a hot chip from Rob's plate and bit down into it with obvious relish. "How's work goin', anyway?"

Pete was a plumber by trade and set his own hours. Ever since their school days, he'd told Rob that he was nuts for going into the corporate world, unable to imagine himself in it. But Rob had felt drawn to law and had proven a natural knack for it.

"Yeah," Rob responded as he lifted the falling apart remains of his burger to his lips, "not bad." Pete raised his eyebrows and Rob shrugged. "Just starting to feel antsy, is all. Think I need a short break." He picked up his beer and sipped at it, staring over Pete's shoulder through the window behind him. Once again, the cloudless blue sky and lush green grass of the outside world seemed to taunt him. "Considering camping out in the pine forest for a while." He shifted his gaze back to Pete's as he set his beer down to pick up a couple of chips. "Wanna come with?"

"Ah, mate, I can't."

Rob scoffed, "I didn't even give you a date, numb nuts."

His friend scratched the back of his neck, the pale, freckled skin of his face turning red. "Yeah, well, right now, things at home are a bit..."

"A bit..?"

Pete exhaled. "Bec and I are...y'know." He made a vague hand gesture which Rob couldn't interpret for love or money.

Cocking his head, his lips twisting up in amusement, Rob said, "I really don't." He reached for his glass again. "Fighting? Taking dance lessons? Planning a holiday? Buying a pub?"

"...trying for a baby."

Rob choked on his beer. "*What?*" he coughed. "Didn't you only just get married, like, a year ago?"

"Three," Pete drummed his fingers atop the worn timber which separated them. "How'd you forget that? You were Best Man and all."

Rob shrugged. "I was exaggerating, you twat. Three years is still early days."

His best friend levelled him with a look, bright blue eyes piercing and serious. "Mate, I've just turned thirty-three 'n she's turning thirty next year. We don't want to leave it much longer." Pete fiddled with the corner of his paper napkin. "Especially not if we decide to have more than one."

"*More...?*" Rob tried not to sound horrified or judgemental. But the very thought of his best friend having kids gave him hives. It made him put his own life into perspective, and that wasn't fun. He forced a grin, reminding himself to be supportive. "Wow. Pete. Mate. That's...*wow.*"

Was it wrong that he felt a little jealous? Not necessarily of Pete (fuck; he had no plans for children of his own. Not now, not ever) but of Pete's potential kid. Kids, even. Because already in the years since his best friend had gotten married, their 'boys' trips' had dwindled down from spontaneous, frequent adventures to occurring once in a blue moon. Pete having kids would likely be the death knell for the trips altogether.

"I know you're not a kid person," Pete laughed, shaking his head in the same fond way he had over the mess on Rob's plate, "but I'm hoping you'll enjoy being Uncle Rob when the time comes. You can even sugar the little monsters up and give 'em back to me all hyper and shit."

Seeing just how excited his friend was at the prospect of being a dad, Rob found he couldn't sulk too much. He cracked a genuine grin and held up his pint. "To you being a dad," he offered as brightly as he could.

Pete's glass clinked against his own. "To you being an honorary uncle!"

Rob drank deeply and glanced back out the window. He definitely needed to get out of the city.

* * *

Rob found that organising the camping trip was relatively easy. Being his own boss came with some perks, after all. He asked his PA to reschedule his meetings for a week or so, passed on any urgent tasks to a couple of the other lawyers under his employ, and then packed up his camper trailer and Toyota Land Cruiser with everything he needed for some time off the grid. Then he called his sister to let her know he mightn't have phone reception for a while.

"You're burning out, aren't you?" Belinda asked him, her voice echoing as it came through the speaker of his phone.

Rob's phone was set off to the side while he typed away at his laptop, frowning. He was multitasking, staying back late in his office in order to send off some emails so that he wasn't leaving a mess for his staff in his absence.

"No," he responded, instantly feeling guilty for being so curt. His fingers paused over the keyboard. "Well, maybe a little."

Lindy (she'd established early on in their childhood that she would *never* answer to 'Belle' as a shortening of her name) was silent for a moment. Rob sensed that his sister was itching to tell him he had bitten off more than he could chew. They'd argued about his career plan many times. She was also a lawyer - criminal law, where he was in contract law - but was much happier working for a corporation, whereas he had always wanted to climb the ranks and be the person holding all the power…and money.

Rob knew that, at thirty-four, he was young for his position. Some had told him he was too young to have his own firm. But he'd proven them wrong. Between his natural talent for the job, his tenacity, and his keen judge of character when hiring similarly-minded staff, his business had flourished in the eighteen months since its launch. But it was stressful and exhausting, and, yes, Lindy had warned him that he might come to regret diving in so deeply, so quickly.

But, when she spoke, she blindsided him by asking, "Is this about Janey?"

"Janey?" Rob echoed, forgetting his half-written email completely. He sat back heavily against the leather of his office chair. "The fuck?"

"It's just, *y'know*…you haven't dated anyone since and you've become even more of a workaholic, and-"

"Janey and I are still friends, Linds." Why his sister couldn't understand that concept, he'd never know. "The breakup was amicable. And I've always been a workaholic."

The sound she made over the line was dismissive. "So…you've just become worse because you're not getting any pussy now?"

Cringing at her vulgarity, he rubbed a hand over his face, feeling the five o'clock growth on his jawline scratching at the skin of his palm. *"Really?"* It wasn't the wording so much as the fact that it was coming from his sister.

He could picture her smug grin. They were far too alike, despite being almost four years apart in age. "Just calling it as I see it, little brother."

"I'm guessing Fiona's not there to smack you upside the head." Belinda's fiancé was a force to be reckoned with. Rob thought it had something to do with the fact that her chosen profession was wrangling six-year-olds on a daily basis as a primary school teacher. "She'd wash your mouth out with soap for that."

"Nah, she likes what I do with my mouth."

"Urgh!" He'd walked himself into her filthy comment. "I don't need those pictures in my head, Belinda. And I don't *want* them there, either."

Her cackling laughter followed; it was infectious. Rob laughed and shook his head while his sister's tone softened. She then said, "It's good to hear you laugh." There was another pause. "I'm glad you're taking a break. It'll be good for you. Even if it's not going to clear the cobwebs off your dick."

Groaning, he cast his gaze to the ceiling. "I should probably be more disturbed that my sister is so keenly invested in my sex life."

"I'm invested in your happiness," she argued back. "And sex… companionship, even…is a huge part of that. Endorphins and lack of loneliness and all that jazz."

Snorting, he sassed, "So eloquent. Have you considered leaving your day job?"

"Robert." Her playfulness had faded away. He envisioned the flat look on her face to accompany her no-nonsense tone. "I know you. You've never been the lone wolf type."

That was true. Admittedly, Rob liked being one half of a relationship. As much as he knew he didn't want kids, he did like being loved and loving in return. Having a partner to enjoy life with was nice. And, off the back of his lunchtime revelation, he could acknowledge he wasn't as needy a friend when he had a girlfriend to entertain…and be entertained by. Life was all about balance, and he wasn't impervious to the fact that he was currently sitting with his backside on the ground and the other side of his metaphorical see-saw empty in the air.

"I'm not disagreeing with you," he responded, "and I'll admit I've been a bit too focussed on work lately. But," he held up his index finger, despite the fact that she couldn't see him, "I'm already taking steps to fix it. Step one: camping. Becoming one with nature. Resetting my chi, or whatever."

Now it was her turn to snort. "Step two?"

"I'll get my arse back on Tinder when I'm back from my trip."

"Good boy."

"Can we change the subject now?" He didn't care that the request was made with a plaintive whine.

Laughing, his sister agreed and did so instantaneously. "So, that blogger I follow wrote this hilarious piece about unexpected uses for shaving cream. There are some hacks in there which actually sound useful…if they work."

"And are these 'hacks' things which could be achieved through products you already have at home?"

This conversation was easier. Rob appreciated that Lindy had dropped the original subject and allowed him the opportunity to tease her instead. His sister, despite being a real shark in the courtroom, was secretly addicted to clickbait. He thought it was hilarious and often told her as much.

Her silence was all the answer he needed.

"You're going to try the shaving cream anyway, aren't you?"

Her laughter was infectious. "Seriously, though, I'll send you the link to the article. The way this woman writes is funny as fuck."

"Is this the same one who wrote that piece which inspired your cobbled together coffee table?" Belinda had convinced Fiona to allow her to build a coffee table out of random Kmart items. The fact that Fiona had gone along with it only proved their relationship was the epitome of True Love (capitals and all) as far as Rob was concerned.

His sister snorted. "Nah, but same site. This is the woman who wrote that hilariously scathing article ranking the various Toms in Hollywood."

"Ah, *her.*" The post in question had been a funny article, actually. She'd ranked Hiddleston as the 'Top Tom', closely followed by Holland and then Hanks. Hardy had been ranked somewhere in the middle. Cruise at the bottom. There'd been more, of course, but Rob didn't really follow celebrities so most of the names had gone over his head. But the writing had been witty, imaginative, and entertaining. He suspected his sister had some sort of crush on the writer. "Send it through."

"I will, and you'll have to tell me what you think!"

He agreed. They said their goodbyes soon after, and Rob then turned his attention back to his emails. One of his clients, Fiona's brother, was still negotiating terms for supplying goods to a grocery giant, so he flagged it as being his first priority once he returned and made himself some notes for information he needed to follow up.

Stefan, who would technically become his brother-in-law once their sisters married, had a farm a few hours' drive away on the outskirts of Stanthorpe. He was going through a rough patch following his own breakup and the dissolution of the business partnership which had been tangled up with the relationship. Rob considered that it might be worth heading out to the farm once the paperwork was ready, not only to go through the contracts in person, but to check on his friend.

A few nights in the cosy cabin he usually stayed in would be the cherry on top.

Gettin' ahead of yourself, mate, Rob mused as he looked over his calendar. *Enjoy camping first before you look for your next escape.*

Still, despite his rational thoughts, he blocked off a few days in his schedule anyway.

Just in case.

＊＊＊

The pine forest was glorious in spring. The tightly packed trees kept most of the heat of the sun away yet allowed plenty of light to filter through their spindly branches. The air was crisp, clean, and earthy, and the very moment Rob climbed out of his driver's seat and took a deep breath, it calmed him.

With the tension in his shoulders already beginning to melt away, he made short work of unhitching the trailer and setting up his camper. He'd spent extra on a model which unfolded itself with the click of a button (needing very little manual intervention to finalise the whole process), making set up and pack down a breeze. Pete had initially mocked Rob for it, telling him that he was no longer camping, but 'glamping'…and yet it hadn't prevented the other man from enjoying the spoils of a quick and easy camping experience on more than one occasion.

With the annex and his camp kitchen set up soon after, there was little left to do but settle in and relax. It was only mid-morning, there were no other souls around, and the only sounds he could hear were those of the birds, the rustling of the trees, and the distant sound of running water from the creek.

Dropping into his reclining camp chair, he checked his watch and thought that eleven o'clock was a perfectly reasonable time to crack open a beer and then have a snooze. He'd go fishing later, and then repeat the whole process every day until his time ran out.

With his eyes drooping shut, Rob sighed and allowed the sounds of nature to lull him off to sleep.

Given himself permission to feel boneless and relaxed was definitely the best idea he'd had in months.

Chapter Four

Livvy was Rosie's best friend and had been since their first year of university. She was tall and reed thin, with gorgeous dark auburn hair and a smattering of freckles across her pale skin which looked almost deliberate and completely adorable. She had sharply intelligent hazel eyes, and a natural charisma that had people (Rosie included) opening up to her with their life stories within hours of meeting her. The two women had bonded over their mutual lamentations of a lackadaisical professor and had soon become inseparable.

After graduating, Livvy had taken an internship with a local news network, and she was employed writing copy for their nightly news program. It was serious - often actual investigative - journalism and there were times where Rosie was more than a little jealous of her friend's success, even though she was also incredibly proud of her.

Livvy was someone Rosie could trust to be brutally honest with her, and yet also temper her honesty with compassion and support. As Rosie had previously mused, her bestie was one of those rare people she could go months without contacting and yet never feel awkward with or feel the need to apologise for the time lost between catchups.

So, when Rosie opened her door to greet Liv in that night, she let out a juvenile squeal of delight and pulled her in for a huge hug. "Seriously, bitch, did you get taller?" she asked with affection as they separated.

The other woman laughed and shook her head, swishing her glorious mane of thick, straight hair like something out of a *L'Oreal* commercial. "I don't think so, but stranger things have happened, right?" Not waiting for an answer, she held up a canvas grocery bag. "Either way, I come bearing gifts of a snack-like nature."

"I accept this as your payment for entering my illustrious lounge room." She watched as Livvy plonked herself on the couch, kicking off her sensible flats and drawing her legs underneath her on the plush seat. "Wine?"

"Always."

"Okay, well, entertain me while I sort this stuff out then." The shorter of the two women instructed as she turned towards the kitchenette, pulling out the fixings for a nice cheese board from the fridge and cupboards. She tilted her head back to glance at her friend. "What have you been up to?"

"It's confidential," Olivia teased. Rosie's eyes widened with intrigue before she feigned offence at the non-answer. Being on the more serious end of the industry, Liv was always privy to secrets, scandals, and otherwise embargoed information. More often than not, though, she'd let her friend in on the information before it hit the news, knowing Rosie wasn't going to scoop her for the story.

"Okay, hit me." Rosie poured them each a glass of sauvignon blanc.

"I really can't this time. It's a big political thing."

Rosie snorted inelegantly, handing over Livvy's glass. "Wait, are we talking State or Federal politics here?"

"Federal." Liv confirmed while Rosie returned to the kitchen for the cheese board.

"Huh." She set the platter of cheese, grapes, crackers, and quince paste down on the coffee table and sat down on the other end of the couch, tucking one leg underneath her. "That juicy, eh?"

Livvy smirked over the rim of her glass, sipping with exaggerated primness. "Uh huh."

"You're killing me here!" Rosie could only watch as her friend stretched the moment out, having set down her wine to prepare a bite of food. If Rosie had been standing, she would have stomped her foot. "Livvy!" she half-laughed, half-whined.

Through a mouth full of double cream brie and crackers, Livvy explained, "I'm sorry. But...I really don't want anyone getting wind of it before it's published. Plus, there's potential to be sued, so..."

"Yeah, yeah, okay." Rosie waved her off. "Who'm I gonna tell, though?"

The redhead shrugged, reaching for another cracker, slathering it with the quince paste and then topping it with brie. She popped it into her mouth and chewed, her eyes closed in a brief moment of food-induced bliss. "No one, I know. But...there might be jail time for the people involved-" Rosie's eyes widened "-so I'm treading lightly."

"You have too much faith in our justice system," Rosie waggled an accusatory grape at her friend before tossing it into her mouth and biting down. She relished the pop of the skin and the burst of sweetness on her tongue. "It's a politician, yeah? Best case, they'll languish in an upmarket, high security prison for maybe six months before they're off on good behaviour. Still," she held up her glass in salute, "congratulations on breaking what sounds like it'll be one of the biggest news stories of the year."

"Thanks." Livvy accepted the toast in her honour and clinked her glass against Rosie's before they both took an obligatory sip. "So, what have you been doing for fun?"

Rosie involuntarily laughed, wondering whether her tragic walk down memory lane qualified as *fun*. "Well," she hedged, focusing on the brie as though it could explain what the hell she was trying to achieve, "I'm writing a longer piece." Liv immediately cheered, and Rosie smiled, bolstered. "It's kind of for work and also...not."

Her friend made a 'continue' gesture with a couple of rolls of her wrist.

Rosie sighed. "It's basically a time-capsule piece, a re-tread over past relationships and crushes."

"Oh!" Livvy's eyes lit up with understanding. "So spill. What's gone wrong so far?"

Rosie was reaching for another cracker but straightened up and glared. "What makes you think anything's gone wrong?"

Livvy gave her a look that spoke of how well they truly knew each other. "You honestly think you can BS me on this? I know you, Weiss. I was there when you tried, and failed, to lie to Professor Montgomery about the 'missing' page of your final thesis for Feminist Literature." She adopted a whiny tone, imitating a younger Rosie, *"Oh, but I know I had it there. It was all bound by the paperclip. Where's the paperclip?"*

Rosie threw a grape at her as she cackled maniacally. "I do not sound like that! Also, it would have totally worked if *you* hadn't started laughing!"

The taller woman grinned back, completely unrepentant. She picked up the attack grape and ate it with blatant enjoyment, settling back against the armrest of the couch. "It would not have worked because he dealt with lying university kids day in and day out. And if you hadn't left it until the last second, you would have finished the paper on time and not had to resort to theatrics."

"Theatrics?" Rosie repeated with widened eyes and a hand to her chest, but her lips curved upwards into a grin which belied the sentiment of her argument. "You bitch! It wasn't theatrics. It was a carefully measured out plan which *would* have bought me an extra day to finish the essay."

"Face it, it was a play right out of your brother's handbook."

And it had been, but Rosie wasn't admitting anything. She would go to the grave playfully blaming her friend for her fail on the assignment - it had become an ongoing, personal joke between the two of them. She sniffed, "Micah's not smart enough to think of something like that."

Livvy tossed her head back with a laugh. "Actually, I buy that much. But he's pretty."

"Don't you start. Grant's got the monopoly on the whole 'Rosie has a hot brother' thing."

"How is Captain Dickwad, anyway?" Livvy was not a fan of Grant and hadn't been since they'd first met. He was too polished and arrogant for her, instantly rubbing her the wrong way, despite Rosie's assurances that he was actually a nice guy. Needless to say, Rosie avoided having her two closest friends interact wherever possible.

Rosie rolled her eyes. "Child," she admonished. "He's pretty good. Actually, he suggested I should take a break, have a holiday and look after myself."

Livvy set down her glass, narrowing her eyes. "Why? What's wrong?"

"There's nothing *wrong*, per se..."

"You're lying again."

"And you're a walking, talking lie detector now, are you?"

"That's deflection."

Rosie huffed and folded her arms across her chest. "There's honestly nothing wrong. I'm just in a bit of a rut, is all."

"Oh, so nothing's wrong except *everything* is wrong?"

"How is it you keep accusing me of being the dramatic one?"

Livvy refilled their glasses again after having emptied the first bottle of wine for the evening. "Start at the beginning," she instructed, once again ignoring her friend's prevarication, seeing it for what it was.

So Rosie did. She explained the original, *completely harmless*, article idea, her brother's reaction, and her determination to prove him wrong. This, naturally, led to confessing the copious amount of wine she'd had to drink during that first night (had it really only been a few days earlier?) and her accidental drunk message to her first boyfriend. Her cheeks flamed red as she handed over her phone when Livvy demanded it, cringing at the laughter accompanying Livvy's reading of the Message of Doom.

"Did you go on that date?" Livvy asked, handing the phone back, her eyes sparkling with mirth.

"It wasn't a date. It was a catch up." Rosie corrected her and then sighed. "But, yeah, I did."

"My brilliant powers of deduction tell me it was *not* a roaring success."

"Gasp!" Rosie held her hand to her chest. "How do you do it?" The question was overtly sarcastic. "No, it sucked." She started listing the reasons on her fingers. "It sucked when I got there, it sucked when I apologised for how I broke up with him, which is another story for another day, and it sucked when he threw a drink in my face for daring to not want to pursue a relationship with him."

"He...*what?!*" Livvy's eyes were wide, her lips twitching. She was visibly torn between amusement and outrage. "Who does that? I mean, outside of bitches in rom-coms or those people you see on Kiss Cam fails."

Rosie shrugged. What more was there to say?

"Oh, Rose, what a palaver," Livvy lamented, flopping back against the couch.

Snorting at her friend's choice of words, Rose reached for the almost empty wine bottle and meted them out another portion each until the bottle ran dry. "Palaver, Liv? Spending time with your grandma again?" A cushion came soaring her way, but she ducked it easily.

"I'll have you know that I have an extensive vocabulary."

"Good for you." Rosie raised her glass as though she were giving another toast. "Now when you're ready to climb down off your high horse and join the rest of us plebs in normal conversation, I'll be waiting."

"What, no stable analogies?"

"You just wanted to use the word 'analogies' just then, didn't you?"

Liv snickered, "You got me."

"You're such a dork."

"You love me."

Rosie tilted her head in acknowledgement. "My sister from another mister."

"And *I'm* the dork." Olivia rose from the couch a little unsteadily, given the entire bottle of wine she'd already consumed, and ambled into the kitchen on her long legs, reminding Rosie of a gangly colt taking its first steps. "How is the rest of your family doing?" Liv asked while she stuck her head into the fridge in the search for another bottle of the good stuff. "You haven't bitched about Micah or your mother at all yet. Are they even still alive?"

"Yeah. Micah's been quiet these last couple of days. He's up to something," Rosie shrugged. "And my mother has also been silent and strangely non-combative. Something's not right."

"That *is* odd." Livvy agreed as she dropped back onto the couch, making a little 'oop' sound as the wine in the newly opened bottle in her hand sloshed around and spilled out a little down the bottle's neck. "What about your dad?"

"He's got his birthday thing tomorrow, so as far as I'm aware he's good." She shrugged, unable to drop the subject of her brother. "Micah said he 'has news' to give us tomorrow, too, so I hope he's not going to ruin Dad's birthday."

The taller woman set the bottle down on the coffee table and scooped up another mouthful of cheese and cracker. "You're not your brother's keeper, Rose. Be like Elsa. Let it go." She ducked as Rosie attempted to swat at her.

"Great. Now that'll be stuck in my head. Thanks."

"You're welcome." Liv's response was cheeky before she steered the conversation back to where they'd started. "So, anyway, you had a disastrous non-date and are now in a rut?"

"Pretty much," Rosie confessed before she could think better of it and picked up her glass again. "Cheers to me."

"I hate to say this," Olivia's expression twisted in distaste, "But I think Captain Dickwad is right. You need a holiday."

Rosie couldn't contain the laughter which bubbled over. "Which would have been way more convincing if you'd called him by his actual name."

"Baby steps, Rose. Baby steps. And, hey, at least you've got your dad's party. That should be fun, yeah?"

Rosie nodded her agreement.

After all, what could possibly go wrong at a family birthday affair?

* * *

Everything. *Everything* could go wrong.

From the second she stepped into the restaurant, it started. As expected, her mother looked her up and down and sighed dramatically, "You couldn't have made an effort? It's his seventieth birthday, sweetheart. And you've not been following your diet plan either, have you?"

There was no use protesting or declaring that this was her 'making an effort' because doing as much would only be poking the bear. And, no, she hadn't been following the diet plan because fuck that noise. She was happy in her skin. Instead, she pasted on a forced smile, kissed her mother on the cheek, and threw her brother under the proverbial bus. "Well," she explained, "I was just *so* excited that Micah has some sort of news to tell us all tonight."

At her side, he glared at her, but she was more than happy to literally shove him into their mother's waiting arms and go in search of her much more mellow father. As she milled through the assembled guests, she could hear her mother needling her brother ("But, darling, you should always tell me your news before anyone else. I spent nineteen and a half hours in labour with you. And I needed stitches. *Stitches*, Micah!") and chuckled darkly to herself.

Her father, Isaac, was seated at the head of the table in the private room which had been booked for the occasion, in conversation with one of his colleagues. He was an accountant by trade and had yet to retire despite Rosie's mother's nagging (or probably *because* of her nagging) and actually seemed to enjoy both his job and the company he kept there. He looked good for seventy, she mused, ever the daddy's girl. Isaac's dark curly hair, the genetic bane of her own existence, had only just begun to turn salt and pepper grey, and he was still as fit and healthy as he'd been in his prime. He looked up as she approached and smiled. "Hello, princess."

Rosie had gone through a period in her teens and early twenties where the epithet had driven her crazy, but she was back to appreciating the affection behind it. "Hey, Dad. Happy Birthday," she greeted, bending to peck kisses to his cheeks. "Having fun?"

"We don't need to go to all this fuss," he told her, inclining his head and gesturing to the grandeur of the space around them, "but if it makes your mum happy, then I'm happy."

Yeah, she thought, *because it means less nagging*. What she said instead was, "Well then I'm glad."

Deciding it was safest to just stay by her father's side, Rosie took up the spare seat to his right, despite knowing that her mother would land to his left, and lost herself in boring accountant conversations. After another fifteen minutes, guests were all seated, the prearranged entrees were being served and the speeches began. Rosie was glad for all of these distractions, because they all prevented her mother from picking up where they'd left off.

It was during dessert, after *Happy Birthday* and *For He's A Jolly Good Fellow* had been belted out of tune and off-key, as they were all digging into cake when Micah stood up (from down at the far end of the table, the rat fink) and clinked his spoon on his glass.

"So, firstly, I'd like to wish Dad a happy seventieth once again," the actor began, raising his glass to his father amid a round of cheers and echoed sentiment, "but I'd also like to announce that I've just gotten the offer of a lifetime."

Rosie could feel the smile slipping from her face.

"I submitted a video audition for a TV series in the States a few weeks ago, and my agent heard back last week. They loved me and they've offered me the role. They've already cast a couple of other well-known actors and feel like the network will pick it up after the pilot. I know I shouldn't be getting ahead of myself, but–"

Whatever he said next was drowned out by their mother's exuberant wailing, and everyone else's well wishes and cheers of support. Phrases like "Nonsense, be confident" and "You'll be amazing" were being shouted over the top of one another and Rosie couldn't hear, couldn't *breathe*, couldn't stand to be in the room any longer. She pushed her chair back, unnoticed because everyone had gotten to their feet to swarm her brother with hugs and pats on the back, slipped out of the room and made her way into the main restaurant. She didn't want to be in that space either, so left the building altogether and wandered aimlessly down the street in the cool air.

Rosie was happy for her big brother but felt hurt that he hadn't forewarned her. Jealousy simmered in her veins, too; a feeling she just couldn't shake. She made it a few hundred metres before she had calmed enough to turn around and head back towards the party. Her father emerged from the front door of the restaurant just as she was reaching to open it, causing Rosie to stumble back in surprise.

Isaac reached out to steady her, softly stating, "Your brother has no class, Rosemary."

The words were enough to tug the corners of her lips upwards. She was relieved, on some level, that she was still his favourite, even if they weren't as close as they'd once been. She was also sort of pleased to realise that while her father couldn't care less about the flashy party held in his favour, he still thought it was poor taste for Micah to hijack it.

She'd been silent too long for his liking, though, so he continued, "But it won't be the same without him, will it?"

For all that she declared they were chalk and cheese, Micah and Rosie were kindred souls. And, sure, she bitched about him constantly, lamented his lack of understanding of her personal space and threatened to revoke his key to her apartment, but she never truly meant any of it. Hell, he'd been absent for maybe three days, and she'd begrudgingly had to admit she had missed him.

What was she going to do with him halfway across the planet?

Her father looked at her warmly. He could always tell when she was spiralling, even if it was internally. He placed his hand on her shoulder and she felt her thoughts begin to settle.

"I'm going camping tomorrow," the declaration left her, seemingly apropos of nothing as they made their way back into the restaurant and to their private party room.

Isaac raised his eyebrows, understandable curiosity splashed across his expression. Rosie didn't much like camping. The bugs. The hard floor. The public bathrooms…or the digging of one's own toilet. But her calendar was empty, and she needed something to jolt her out of her funk. This wasn't exactly what Grant had meant by 'take a holiday', but she had just committed to the idea.

"It'll probably be a little three-day thing, but I'm excited." She fought the urge to facepalm as the words left her mouth. She couldn't even fake it. Why would she say such a thing?

Her dad's smile was soft and understanding without being condescending. "It'll be good for you to step back for a minute. It might lend you some perspective."

Rosie didn't really know what he meant by 'lending some perspective', but her father wasn't a particularly chatty guy. She let it pass.

Eventually her mother and brother returned to the table, still cooing over Micah's big break. Rosie stood and gave her brother a big hug.

"I'm proud of you. Congratulations." She was proud of *herself* for being able to say it convincingly through the pang of resentment she still felt. But, she supposed, she did genuinely feel happy for Micah's success.

Her brother deserved all the happiness in life. For all his faults (and there were many of them) he was a good soul.

Micah's answering smile practically lit up the room. How he'd managed to keep his secret under wraps, she'd never know. "Thanks, Rose."

God, she could not wait to escape.

Chapter Five

"Why the ever-loving fuck did I ever think this was a good idea?" Rosie asked herself as she struggled to assemble her tent. Her expression twisted into a self-deprecating sneer while she adopted a falsetto, mocking herself. *"Oh, I'm going camping for a few days."* In frustration, she threw the tent peg in her hand to the ground. "Next time, I'm booking a penthouse suite at a swanky hotel. Fuck this shit."

Rich laughter broke through her rant. She jumped in surprise, spinning to find the source of the sound leaning against a nearby tree. It was a man - dark haired, and stormy-eyed with artfully trimmed stubble across his delightfully angular jawline - grinning at her with blatant amusement.

"You right?" he asked, unrepentant at having been caught revelling in her misery.

"I'm regretting every single one of my life choices, actually," she responded testily, feeling the burn of a blush on her cheeks. "But, yeah, I'm fine."

He didn't appear at all convinced. "Really?"

There was a part of her which wanted to tell him that if he began mansplaining how to set up a tent, he might just discover that she knew other places she could wedge a tent peg. However, at the same time, she was actually struggling and could probably use the help, her broken pride be damned.

With her shoulders sagging, the fight left her, and she shook her head, "No.

Turns out I'm actually really shit at this."

"I wasn't going to say anything," he responded lightly, pushing off the tree and sauntering forward. As he neared, she refused to acknowledge that he was quite handsome. She resolutely did not check out how well his jeans moulded to his butt (she truly didn't) and *did not* notice how he smelled absolutely *divine*. He stuck out his hand by way of introduction, "Rob."

"Rosie," she told him, accepting the handshake.

He smiled warmly. "Nice to meet you, Rosie." And, before the awkwardness could set in, he gestured around them, "This your first time setting up camp on your own?"

He could have very well have been a predator, but she couldn't treat every person she came across as a threat, even though admitting she was camping alone was a stupid move which went against everything she'd ever been taught. Still, she found herself nodding, "Yeah. Like I said, regretting all my life choices right now."

This, at least, earned her another of those deep, rich laughs from the man. Rob.

*Which, hey, might not even be his real name. He could be a psychopath or a serial killer, but **what** a way to go...*

She shook her head free of the dangerous path her thoughts were travelling down. Had she not recently learned her lesson? Besides, this delicious specimen was more than likely spoken for. Especially if he was genuinely a good Samaritan type.

"And what brings a city girl like you camping on her own?" he asked, thankfully ignorant of her internal monologue as he moved towards her tent.

"It's a long story," she shrugged. "A knee-jerk reaction to a whole lot of crap going on, I guess."

Rob gave her a friendly smile, the tiny cleft in his chin more prominent with the action. "Oh, yeah?" he asked with a warmth which was instantly disarming.

This, of course, saw Rosie internally bracing herself, specifically to save herself the embarrassment of inevitably putting her foot in her mouth.

Still, a reply was necessary, and she surprised herself when the words tumbled forth with unbridled honesty. "My brother is moving overseas to pursue his dreams, and it just shines this big spotlight on everything I'm not achieving."

Her newfound companion's expression turned a little stunned, and it was obvious that he hadn't been expecting such a deep and meaningful answer to leave her lips either. She grabbed the rest of her issues and shoved them into a metaphorical pigeonhole labelled *'Not Today'*, including the footnote explaining that this feeling of not accomplishing anything began gestating months ago: prior to Micah effing off to America and prior to her big, still painful breakup.

"Really?" Rob asked, looking her and her possessions over, "you seem successful enough to me." His observation sliced through her thoughts and brought her back to reality. To which Rosie thought to herself, *'How and why is camping my reality?!'*

Wait, was that a compliment? Did the pretty guy who may or may not be a murderer just awkwardly compliment her? Or was he only making conversation with the emotional time bomb he'd accidentally stumbled across?

So lost in overanalysing everything, she missed her opportunity to offer witty repartee. Filling the silence, Rob arched his eyebrows and added, "Except, y'know, when it comes to setting up camp."

Charming, she thought with sarcasm. *No,* she argued with herself (a sure sign she was truly losing her mind), *he's **genuinely** charming. This guy is gonna build my tent like I'm a Disney princess.*

She might have been a feminist, strong willed and independent, but she could accept help where it was offered and admit when she needed it. Besides, just because she'd had a shit run with other members of his gender recently did not mean she should paint this man with the same brush.

"Thank you," she finally said aloud, smiling at her newfound friend. In less than ten minutes, the tent was erect, and Rosie had her home for the next couple of nights.

Given his stunned reaction to her previous oversharing, she was reticent to say much of anything else outside of small talk. Instead, she asked about him.

It turned out Rob was also camping alone, which seemed a bit of a travesty given how friendly and attractive he was…but also fed into her paranoia that he was a serial killer. He told her he was going fishing soon and he would be staying at a site not far from hers until the end of the weekend. She doubted she would make it the three days, but this was a strong start.

Rob looked at his work with satisfaction. Rosie fought the urge to tell him that he had done his good deed for the day.

"Well," he declared as he dusted his hands off on his jeans, "if I catch enough fish, I'd love to cook you dinner."

This declaration startled a laugh out of Rosie. He couldn't be serious. But the disheartened look which flitted across his face implied Rob hadn't been joking.

She quickly offered him a smile, barely restraining herself from reaching out to put a conciliatory hand on his tanned forearm, "That would be great."

Rob smiled, nodded, and headed back to his campsite, tossing a jovial "It's a date!" back over his shoulder as he left.

After he left, Rosie grabbed a pillow and laid in the sunlight with a book, her focus on the words becoming distracted by the trees, the sounds of the nearby lake, and the recent memory of Rob.

Was this the start of something, or was she crushing on the first guy to give her any semblance of affection? Or was it just because he was very pretty and friendly, so some primal part of her had just decided he was an acceptable mate? Or was she just trying to avoid focusing on her personal issues, using this new, chiselled creature with the boyish smile, practically handed to her on a silver platter by fate herself, as a perfect distraction?

She huffed at the last turn her thoughts had taken, wondering why it was so hard for people to just be upfront and honest about their intentions.

Because, her inner monologue supplied, which to her utmost irritation sounded a lot like her brother, **you** *never are*.

Damn it. Her stupid brother (or his voodoo ghost that had followed her here) was indeed right.

* * *

Later that day Rosie experienced a bizarre moment, an odd emotion coiling in her belly. It felt like dread, but not serious dread. Not 'stalker-ex-acting-out-slasher-fantasies' dread, but instead the basic 'please-don't-let-me-be-humiliated' kind of dread. Rosie didn't know anything about the former kind, but she imagined it was a more serious affair. Instead, she was just feeling socially awkward.

The issue? Rosie had *no* idea what her camping beau's name was. He had introduced himself, helped set up her tent, and somewhere between ogling his butt as he'd sauntered away earlier in the day and waking up from an impromptu nap in the sun, Rosie had forgotten his name.

And, okay, he wasn't *hers*, and he *really* wasn't her beau, so Rosie was happy to silently concede that she needed to reel her crazy back in a little.

Why was this such an issue for her? Because the nice man had returned with four fish in a bucket.

"Joining me for dinner?" he asked, all sun kissed and now deliciously shirtless, because apparently fishing required the removal of one's shirt, as he held up his catch. He had a fine smattering of chest hair, coarse and dark, across defined pectorals leading down a gently toned but not obscenely muscular abdomen.

Dear God, she thought, *I'm officially a lech.* She didn't want to be. Looks weren't everything. But she couldn't help the way her heart rate increased as her eyes - her awful, traitorous eyes - drank him in.

In that moment, she became hyper aware of her own less than stellar appearance: hair in a messy bun; no makeup; a frumpy old t-shirt; and jeans which were beginning to thin just a tad too much in the thigh region because, in her world, thigh gaps were an imaginary construct like Santa, or the Easter Bunny, or winning the lotto. She hadn't anticipated the need to impress anyone here (and a little voice in her head reminded her that there was no need to impress anyone, full stop) but he was just *so. damn. handsome.*

Rosie wanted to slap herself for the circular, redundant thoughts in her head. Had she really been so messed up by life recently that this was what she was reduced to? Feeling guilty for having the gall to appreciate someone's beauty?

And, damn it, she'd been quiet for way too long again.

Pasting on a grin, she nodded and got to her feet. "I'd love you," she said. As quickly as she said them, her ears registered the words. Her cheeks burned and she rushed to correct herself. "To! *To*. I'd love *to*. For fuck's sake." The urge to just crawl into her tent (the tent he'd built her!) and hide was strong. *Smooth, Rosemary. Real smooth.* She shook her head and sighed, avoiding his amused gaze, "Let's write that off on minor heat stroke, okay?"

"Write what off?" he was gentlemanly enough to ask; she felt her stomach give a little lurch at the playful grin which accompanied the question.

He was a saint. She could have kissed him! But that wouldn't have helped with the embarrassment much.

Rosie dusted off leaves and dirt from her jeans, studiously ignoring him. "So, I'm obviously not great at this whole 'roughing it' thing. What kind of fish are those?" She jutted her chin towards the bucket containing his catch.

"Whiting," he answered, and she nodded, more or less because she felt it was the appropriate response.

He chuckled at her knowingly while his eyes glinted with mirth. "That means nothing to you, huh?"

"Not a damn thing," she laughed. "Sorry."

He brushed the apology off. "Kinda' expected as much. All you need to know is they'll taste good when I'm done with 'em."

Rosie bit back a lascivious reply, determined not to embarrass herself further when she couldn't even remember his name. Instead, she offered to help, adding, "But, fair warning, I've never filleted a fish in my life, and if my skill at building a tent is any indication…" Her shoulders lifted and dropped as she trailed off, but she wore an unrepentant grin.

"You can come keep me company?" The nice man suggested by way of compromise.

Not in the least bit insulted, and honestly a little relieved, Rosie agreed to his proposal. "Tell you what: I have wine. That can be my contribution."

"Works for me."

Rosie retrieved the aforementioned beverage. It was in cask form, which she normally turned her nose up at, but it was still Brown Brothers and, when camping, a cask just made more sense. Box of wine in hand, she followed her camping neighbour through the light bush to his site. She whistled approvingly at his set up: a deluxe looking camper trailer and a full camp kitchen. It made her dodgy little one-man tent look positively uncouth in comparison. "Wow."

He seemed chuffed by her approval, ducking his head and attempting a modest deflection, "It's enough for me." He put the bucket of fish down and, in what Rosie wanted to call a criminal act, slipped a fresh flannel shirt on, deft fingers running up the buttons and covering up the beautiful chest and abdomen which had been on display.

Smothering a sigh, Rosie settled herself in his camp chair while he set about cleaning, scaling, and filleting the fish. They made small talk which was actually quite pleasant. She learned he was a lawyer who lived on the Gold Coast, and she joked that if she ever committed a crime, she'd look him up. Of course, to do so would involve remembering his name, and she still hadn't gotten there yet.

"You just don't seem very lawyerly," she informed him a few drinks later, her inhibitions having made their retreat, along with her grasp of the English language. "If you'd said farmer or tradie…"

Thankfully, he didn't seem insulted. He just plated up their meals and sat cross legged on the ground in front of her. "Well, I do know how to shave and wear a suit, too."

Her cheeks warmed. She told herself that it was because of the wine and not the image which had popped into her head. Raising her plastic mug of wine at him in salute, she rallied, "The trademark of a successful lawyer."

Towards the bottom of the cask, the attractive lawyer man (Roger? Ron? Roy? Reg?) regaled her with a tale of the last great fish he'd caught, slipping into colloquialism with his inebriation. His cheeks were a ruddy pink from the alcohol, his grey-blue eyes wide and glinting with excitement while his hands gestured wildly.

"The rod was bowing like crazy, right? An' I'm standing off the back of this tinnie with my whole body weight on this like..." he trailed off and stood, striking a pose, miming the encounter to Rosie's increasing amusement. "And my mate, Pete, goes to grab the net, and he ends up tripping, slicing up his leg. Blood everywhere, and I wanna help him, but this fish is up in the air, flappin' about. Probably three times higher than my head at this point."

Rosie was transfixed by the conversation. She couldn't care less about fishing, however watching him excitedly retell the story with an almost childish enthusiasm was riveting. His passion was a powerful aphrodisiac. Or maybe that was the wine and his flexing biceps, and the little dimple she'd discovered hidden under the scruff on his cheek. Who knew?

"In the end, I get the fish on the boat and Pete starts applying pressure to the gash. After five minutes the towel is full, and the blood isn't stopping-"

In this moment, bile surged to the back of Rosie's throat. She didn't like blood at all, but she needed to know the end of the grisly story. Did this long-winded epic end in Pete's untimely death? Given the broad, boyish grin on her companion's face, she doubted it.

"So, we have to go back to land." His shoulders slumped, his regret almost palpable.

Rosie teased with a scandalised gasp, "Oh no. Not *land!*"

He frowned a little. "When you're on the water you're on the water, you know? It takes forever to come back." Rosie supposed her companion might be insulted that she would think this wasn't a big deal when it was clearly the biggest of deals to him.

Obviously, Rosie did not know quite how it felt, but she nodded to smooth things over. She still thought he was over-exaggerating. After all, it sounded as though Pete had lost a lot of blood and Roland (Ray?) had his fish. She was most certainly on the side of seeking medical attention for the injured friend.

"So, while he was getting seven stitches in his kneecap, I cooked the best catch of my life on a barbecue in the park opposite the medical centre. It was awesome."

Rosie took a sip of her wine after making the appropriate hum of approval and asked, "Where's Pete today?"

To this, her companion let out a huff of breath, trying to stifle his disappointment as best he could. "He was busy this week. His job's picked up and he's trying to save money for when he has a kid."

She brightened the way one was expected to whenever talk of babies was involved. "Oh, how exciting! How far along is his partner?"

With a put-upon sigh, the dark-haired lawyer shook his head, dropping back down to sit at her side. "She's not, actually. Not yet, but they're *trying*, apparently." There was a lilt of frustration which he couldn't quite disguise and which she empathised with. She imagined he felt a little distanced from his friend now, possibly set to the side. Or maybe she was just projecting some of her own issues again. Still, the handsome man shook off his disappointment and his cheeky grin was back. He puffed out his chest. "I'm going to be Uncle Rob."

Rob! This probably-not-a-murderer's name was Rob. *Thank you, wine*, Rosie thought to herself, ticking re-learning his name off her 'to do' list.

And then, emboldened by the reminder of his name, the stars above them, the campfire meal and the entertaining conversation, Rosie leaned over and kissed Rob.

There was a startled moment where she wondered whether she may have misread the entire situation before Rob himself leaned into the kiss, bringing a hand up to cradle the back of her head and draw her further down towards him. It was an awkward kiss, as far as first kisses went, clumsy due to their odd angle and the alcohol, but Rosie still felt a spark of excitement, the thrill of something new and unexpected. She hadn't kissed anyone since her breakup with Damian.

Probably not the best thing to focus on right then.

A little voice at the back of her mind told her that doing this was not the smartest move she could make, especially not when she still wasn't convinced he wasn't a crazy axe-murderer because she knew absolutely nothing about him, but she ignored it. Wasn't the aim of this escape to revel in some freedom and actually enjoy herself? This didn't have to mean anything. She could let loose and have fun. She could.

Admittedly, this wasn't the kind of fun she had been planning on.

"You're overthinking," Rob criticized playfully, pulling away from the kiss and tucking a loose strand of her messy hair behind her ear. "And also, not that I'm complaining, but what just happened here?"

She supposed, given his last words had simply been a declaration of his impending honorary unclehood, her actions might have been a *little* confusing.

"Uh," Rosie floundered. For someone who was great with expressing herself via the written word, she found that her mouth refused to be anywhere near as eloquent.

The ghost of a smile was tugging at the corner of his lips, threatening to draw them into a smirk. "Oh, well *that* explains it." Rob's voice was deep, undeniably masculine and, coupled with his expressive eyes, Rosie was lost to it.

"Sorry," she managed sheepishly, "I just...uh..." she made a vague gesture with her hands.

He laughed, shaking his head. "Yeah, that cleared it right up." His hand was on her thigh, the warmth of his palm searingly distracting.

It took her a few more moments to get the coordination going between her brain and her mouth. Rob was patient, his expression warm and encouraging. She focused on not being tongue-tied.

"Okay, so, I'm new to this," she confessed with a confidence she wasn't entirely certain she felt, but Rob hadn't moved away and that encouraged her to continue. "The flirting not..." she shrugged, trailing off and trying to remember the point she had been trying to make because he was ever so slowly moving the thumb on her thigh. "Anyway, maybe I misread the situation, but...I mean, we're both out here on our own and..."

"And?" he prompted, his voice lower and his eyes darker, or at least this was how Rosie suddenly perceived him.

Her heart rate was increasing; she wasn't sure whether it was with anticipation or embarrassment. A little of both, she figured, feeling out of her depth. *You're a strong, independent woman,* she reminded herself, *there's no shame in being confident and assertive.*

As much as she truly believed all the above, she'd never actually acted purely out of self-interest like this, and she thought maybe *that* was what was causing her to hesitate. Despite having some issues with her body, she knew everyone had issues they were self-conscious about. Hell, she was certain that even the seemingly confident man in front of her probably had his own insecurities. So she had never actually been shy when it came to sex. But this was completely different to being in a committed relationship…and there she went again overthinking matters.

"And I'm not looking for anything serious," she told him, surprising even herself with the brutal honesty of the words but feeling much more secure in the situation once she'd put them out there, "and you seemed as interested in me as I am in you. So, I guess I took the shot."

His lips curled upwards, less boyish grin and more roguish. It suited him, and suddenly Rosie could imagine Rob as a lawyer, more shark than the Labrador puppy she had been interacting with all evening.

"And?" he pressed again, somehow imbuing the word with levels of meaning while his thumb continued to draw distracting patterns on the inseam of her jeans at her thigh. He seemed far too coherent and bright-eyed for someone who'd had half a cask of wine, but then she didn't feel overly drunk either.

Pleasantly buzzed, perhaps. Enough to have the confidence to go through with this.

Whatever *this* ended up being, anyway.

Rosie's answering laugh was breathy. She set her empty cup down in the chair's inbuilt cup holder and rose to her feet, planting her hands on her hips. "And I think maybe you should give me a tour of your abode."

Rob got to his feet gracefully, somehow avoiding the awkward scramble Rosie had always encountered when getting up from the ground. But, instead of eagerly pulling her into the aforementioned shelter, he gave her a searching look. He didn't ask if she was sure, or if she was sober enough to understand what she was doing, but there was a flicker in his expression which suggested he had considered doing so.

Abstractly, she wondered what sort of law he practiced, but the question was pushed aside as he bent towards her and dipped his head down for a kiss which was far less clumsy than the last.

So, no, this mightn't have been the getaway she'd imagined when Grant had encouraged Rosie to take off and enjoy herself, but she was *definitely* enjoying it regardless.

"You've seen the kitchen," Rob teased, gesturing to the camp kitchen out in the annex they'd been sitting in, "and this," he led her up the two little steps to the inside space, "is my combined lounge room and bedroom."

If she'd been paying more attention, Rosie would have taken in the details of Rob's camper. Instead, Rosie glanced over the bench seats to her right and moved towards the 'bed' at her left.

It was obviously much more luxurious than her crappy little camping mattress, though she doubted it would be the most comfortable surface in the world. Still, she wasn't exactly there to examine it for comfort, was she?

With a hip resting against the other end of the bed, Rob smirked. "Satisfied?"

She laughed. "What? Am I supposed to say something corny like 'Not yet, but I'm hoping I will be'?"

"You're a bit of a smart arse, aren't you?" he asked, closing the space between them in one stride. He grinned and reached down to squeeze one of her denim-clad butt cheeks. "But it's a nice arse."

She decided that his cheesy lines could be attributed to the wine, but they were endearing. Unless that was the wine talking to her, too.

"I'm glad you think so," she responded, following his lead and smoothing her hands down the front of his flannel shirt. She offered him a cheeky grin. "You're not so bad yourself."

Rob's return grin was equally playful before he leaned down and kissed her.

His mouth moved against hers with purpose, his tongue poking out to entwine with hers. His scruff felt sharp and prickly against her slightly windburned lips, but, strangely, it only turned her on more.

Rosie's fingers worked at unbuttoning Rob's shirt as their kissing became more heated, and his hands tugged at her t-shirt. They separated long enough for her to pull the loose cotton over her head and toss it somewhere in Rob's so-called 'lounge room'.

She was down to her sports bra -because fuck wearing an underwire bra while she was camping- and jeans, shucking off her sneakers while Rob shrugged off his shirt. She felt a brief moment of uncertainty, comparing her soft, stretch marked, rounded belly to his firm, toned abdomen. But she shook it off at the hungry gaze he directed at her proportionately ample breasts. And, if that wasn't convincing enough, the tenting of his jeans was also reassuring.

Emboldened by his physical reaction, she reached down to fondle his cock through the restrictive denim. Rob sucked in a surprised breath and closed his eyes, rocking into her hand. Leaning forward, Rosie pressed open mouthed kisses to his clavicle and chest. His hands slid up her back, and then his left hand slipped under the band of her bra and sneaked around to her breast.

"Oh," she breathed as he rolled her nipple between his thumb and index finger.

Rob opened his eyes and grinned at her before their lips reconnected in another kiss. This time it was messier, more heated, almost frenzied. Her hands moved to his belt, unbuckling it as best she could while distracted by the way his tongue was working against hers.

She whined as he removed his hand from her breast, now unbuttoning and unzipping her jeans. Then his hands moved to her hips. He curled his fingers into her waistband, and she wiggled from side to side, encouraging him to get on with it.

Rob smirked against her mouth and wordlessly complied, pushing her jeans and underwear down over her hips and thighs. She reciprocated, repeating the same actions on him, and they both completed the awkward manoeuvre of stepping out of their jeans. It was made even more awkward by the cramped space they were working with, but neither of them seemed to care.

In the dimly lit camper, Rosie was disappointed that she couldn't properly take in the details of his form, especially the sizable erection jutting against her stomach. She reached for his cock, stroking it and delighting in the groan the action elicited. Instead of closing his eyes and enjoying her ministrations as he had before, her touch on his hardened flesh seemed to drive him wild. Rob pulled Rosie's bra up, exposing her breasts; his mouth descended upon one, his right hand cupping the other.

She clenched her thighs together, arousal pooling while he continued to fondle and lick and suck. When he moved his mouth to her other breast, his right hand travelled down between her legs, sliding fingers into her folds. He rubbed circular patterns over her clit and there was no way she could describe the sound she made. Rosie widened her stance, inviting him to dip his fingers deeper, inside her.

Rob's cock twitched in Rosie's hand when he encountered how wet she was, precum beading at the tip. Rosie smoothed over the liquid with her thumb, then brought her thumb to her mouth, tasting him.

"Fuck," he practically growled with appreciation, "that's hot."

From beneath coquettish lashes, she smirked back at him. "If you think that's hot, wait 'til you see what I can do with my tongue." And, before he had a chance to tease her back, she shifted their positions, so his butt was resting against the bed, and lowered herself to her knees in front of him.

With his hands threading into her hair, Rob leaned his weight back against the camper's bed. Rosie took only a moment to inspect his dick, which was unsurprisingly as attractive as the rest of him; long and curved slightly, the vein practically throbbing, and the head flushed dark. She took what she could into her mouth. What didn't fit, she wrapped her hand around.

As promised, she twirled her tongue, putting to good use the skills she'd cultivated when she'd taught herself how to knot a lolly snake in her mouth at the age of eighteen. With her free hand, she fondled his balls and, feeling bold, ran a finger over his perineum.

"Christ," he muttered, thrusting in time with her combined stroking and sucking, "more of that, yeah?"

His blatant enjoyment at her hand had her shifting her own hips, searching for friction. She was practically dripping, desperate to feel him inside her. She stopped fondling his balls, moving her hand to her own clit to ease the growing ache.

Rob made a sound of protest, opening his eyes to glance down at her. When he realised what she was doing, he shook his head and gently pulled himself away from her mouth, reaching a hand out to tug her back up onto her feet.

"What?" she asked, but in lieu of an answer, he captured her mouth in a hard, hungry kiss, before he slid his hands under her thighs and seemed to lift her effortlessly. She squealed because she wasn't used to being lifted so easily.

Rob spun around to deposit her on the mattress previously behind him. Then he spread her legs wide and ducked his head between them.

Rosie cried out in equal parts surprise and pleasure as his tongue found her clit with startling accuracy, and then he slid two fingers inside her, which she clenched around instinctively. "Holy shit," she murmured as he worked her to the brink of ecstasy in what felt like seconds, his stubble tickling her skin while his tongue - his glorious, wicked tongue - replaced his fingers. "Fucking *fuck*," she whimpered.

Oral sex had never felt like this before. Sure, she'd enjoyed it on the odd occasion she'd been indulged, but it had always taken her a while to fully relax into it, and even longer to push her over the edge of orgasm. But Rob...he was something else! He seemed to have magic in his fingers and tongue and, *Jesus*, even his damn *nose* – a ridiculous thought, but it genuinely felt as though he was working her to ecstasy with every tool at his disposal. Well, except for the one she was close to begging for.

"Oh," she attempted to verbalise as she felt the tell-tale signs of her orgasm approaching, but the words which came out were, "*God*, right *there*...don't stop!"

Then she was crying out as her thighs shook and pleasure exploded inside her, skittering across all of her nerve endings. It was the most intense orgasm she'd ridden out in years, if ever. She squealed and attempted to clamp her thighs shut as she came down from the high and felt him still lapping at her now over-sensitive flesh.

Rob grinned a Cheshire Cat grin at her, his lips and cheeks glistening in the low lighting, and then he wiped his face directly on the sheet beside him. She was in no state of mind to judge the action.

"Where," she panted, trying to catch her breath, even as she scooted onto the bed properly and made room for him to join her, "where'd you learn to do that? 'Cos that was…" she struggled to describe it. Only two words came to mind. "Pure magic."

His resulting chuckle was low and flirtatious as he stretched out on his side next to her. "A gentleman never reveals his secrets."

"You, sir, are no gentleman," she shot back, reaching for the weeping cock he was now slowly rubbing against her thigh, "and I am so glad you're not." Rob made an unintelligible sound in response, clearly distracted by the way she was stroking him. She bit her lip. "Do you have condoms in here?"

She hadn't really thought this whole 'impromptu sleeping with a stranger' thing out.

Rob nodded. "Yeah." He tilted his head back, eyes shut. "Fuck, I hope they're in date." Then he extricated himself from her hold and rolled over. Rosie couldn't help but squeeze the firm backside he'd presented to her as he leaned over the edge of the bed and rummaged through one of the built-in drawers beneath it. He emerged with a victorious cry, rolling back over with a foil square in his hand. "In date. Thank God."

"I mean, not to get technical," she teased as he tore into the packet and rolled the condom on, "but I think it's more a 'thank Rob of the past' sort of deal."

"Then thank me of the past," he agreed, crawling over her as she spread her thighs for him once more. He slipped in slowly with an appreciative groan that she echoed, and it didn't take them long to fall into rhythm together.

At her urging, Rob thrust harder and faster. Rosie clutched at his biceps as she felt the delicious coil of tension and pleasure tightening inside her again. Then he propped himself on one elbow, reached between them, and dropped his mouth down to hers, sucking on her bottom lip as he rubbed his thumb over her clit. Before she knew it, she flew over the precipice of her second orgasm, clenching around his still pumping cock while the bliss washed over her again.

This time as she came down from her high, she was aware of his hips jerking as he followed her over the edge, coming hard inside her with a muffled groan into her mouth, given that he was still kissing her.

He withdrew slowly, then hopped off the bed to throw the rubbish away. The burst of cool night air through the open camper door brought out a rash of goosebumps across her sweat-slicked skin. Rosie immediately felt awkward because she'd never done this with a complete stranger, but before she could force her jelly legs to roll her off the bed, Rob returned with a sheet and a litre bottle of water.

She watched as he took long gulps from the bottle, his Adam's apple bobbing with the effort before he held it out to her. She did her best to drink demurely, but she was thirsty as hell after their burst of activity. Wiping her mouth on the back of her hand, she passed the half empty bottle back to him and had no idea what to say other than, "Thanks."

"My pleasure," he practically purred, setting the bottle aside and climbing back into the bed, heedless of their nudity. He draped the sheet he'd procured over the top of them.

Rosie blinked in surprise as Rob snuggled up against her, having blocked her escape, and asked, "You want me to stay?"

With half-lidded eyes, the combination of the alcohol and the orgasm clearly enacting a soporific effect on him, Rob kissed her temple and nodded. "It'll be more comfortable than your setup."

She couldn't argue with that logic. Not giving it any more thought, she merely nodded and drifted off to sleep beside him.

Chapter Six

In hindsight, Rosie mused the next morning, biting back a groan when her back complained at the movement of simply waking up, *camping was a stupid idea*.

Camp mattresses sucked. Even the fancy one in Rob's camper trailer proved to be unbearably awful. Sure, waking up tucked against his side with his arm around her was nice, but she felt stiff and sore and not in a 'I've been doing delightfully naughty things' kind of way. She needed a massage. A hot stone massage. And a warm bubble bath. And a mattress which didn't make her feel as though she was sleeping on solid rock.

And she really, *really* needed to pee.

It took some manoeuvring, but she managed to slip from the 'bed' (and she was using that term loosely because what she had slept on had no business masquerading as a bed) without waking her companion, gathered her discarded clothes and ducked into his onsite pop-up ensuite. She turned her nose up as she encountered the portable camp toilet. At least it was better than digging herself a hole, but only marginally. Why had she ever thought camping was the answer to her problems? In that moment, she regretted her life choices all over again.

Well, except maybe the previous night. That had been fun.

She finished up, dressed, and then hovered outside the camper, wondering what the protocol here was. Should she just find her way back to her own campsite now? Should she crawl back into bed with him? Should she get super presumptuous and prepare breakfast? *I thought one-night stands were supposed to be easier,* the voice in her head muttered disparagingly, *but this is most certainly not easier.*

The sound of a throat being cleared shook her from her thoughts. She turned around and looked up to find the very object of her musings observing her with obvious amusement glinting in his eyes. His short dark hair was all tousled and he was wearing low slung flannel pyjama bottoms which looked super soft and comfortable. He seemed completely at ease. "Mornin'," he greeted, his voice gravelly with sleep. "Still overthinking, huh?"

She grinned sheepishly, "Yeah. It's a bad habit." One she'd had her entire life and doubted she'd ever shake.

He meandered over to his camp kitchen and set about getting a kettle on the boil. "Coffee?" he asked, holding up a tin of instant.

Her tastebuds were already complaining, but instant coffee was better than no coffee, and it wasn't as though she hadn't also packed the freeze-dried crap in her own setup. She nodded eagerly. "Please."

"Milk?" he asked, already pulling out the camp fridge on its sliding rack from under the trailer's body.

"Yes. No sugar."

"Sweet enough without it, yeah?" Rosie snorted and he made a face. "Yeah, I heard how lame that was, too," he confessed, still grimacing. "Give me a break, I'm still not caffeinated."

She liked this side of him. Less cocky (not that the confidence hadn't been hot, mind you) and hinting at silly. With his hair at all angles and a pillow crease across his left cheek, he seemed almost younger and sweeter. Also, these were dangerous thoughts. This was not a relationship. She wasn't looking for anything serious. *Abandon ship, Rosemary.*

As they made more small talk while the water boiled, she found herself answering questions about her own life. She told him about her job, about the stupid idea she'd had for the article, and about the disaster that had been her date with Jimmy. She laughed about the drink incident while she accepted a mug from Rob before she closed her eyes and breathed in the aroma. It was soothing, even if it was instant crap.

"So, you had a crappy date and ran into the forest?" Rob summarised after he'd sipped at his own beverage, eyeing her knowingly over his mug. "Because, honestly, that…actually explains a lot."

He was sharper again, and once more she was reminded of his profession. "Well, no, it wasn't just that. There were a bunch of little things which kind of added up to push me over the edge."

"Uh huh."

She swatted at him.

It didn't occur all at once, but over the course of the day Rosie and Rob got to know a lot about each other.

Rosie found herself recounting embarrassing stories about a girls' trip to Bali she'd taken during her uni days, and Rob told Rosie that he was the one who had introduced Pete to his wife a little under five years ago. Micah's sudden success was brought up, with Rosie admitting that she was concerned her brother was uprooting his entire life for 'just a pilot' which might not even be picked up by a network, and Rob solemnly confessed that he'd caught one of the staff at his firm selling information and was forced to let him go. In turn, Rosie admitted that she always worried about her dad's health even though she had no reason to, and Rob informed her that his own father had passed away unexpectedly two years prior.

Conversation flowed easily and confiding in him was freeing. She told herself it was because she didn't know him and had no plans to see him again after this trip. There was no room for a relationship in her life. Not with the state of mind she had been in.

They exchanged numbers but, at the end of the day, Rosie felt claustrophobic. She couldn't quite pinpoint why. She liked Rob. She liked their talks. She didn't feel any pressure from him. Sure, he'd asked to exchange numbers, and he'd been rather tactile, but it wasn't like he was begging her to stay. Her tendency to overthink wasn't helping, she knew that much. But it wasn't something she could just switch off.

Rosie feigned exhaustion and bid Rob goodnight, returning to her own tent with a hint of fear that things were rapidly progressing from 'one-night stand' to 'potential relationship'.

After unloading her worries about Micah onto Rob, Rosie was struck by the urge to call her brother, but she didn't because she foolishly believed she needed to learn how to be without him before he left. Besides, her phone battery was flatter than a pancake.

Over a portable gas camping stove, Rosie quickly cooked some pasta and mixed in spaghetti sauce, despite knowing her tastebuds would have thanked her for another night spent at Rob's campsite. Following her meal, she flicked on the lamp in her tent and climbed into 'bed' to read a good book. Her back would have appreciated the other faux bed better too, she mused, but even so she longed for her mattress at home.

As much as she tried, Rosie couldn't concentrate on the words on the pages in front of her. Her brain was too busy. She'd had a one-night stand. This was something she'd never done before. She still had no idea on protocol. She liked Rob. In another life, she could see herself pursuing a relationship with him, but deep down Rosie knew that she did not need to add to her issues by throwing herself headfirst into dating again.

But out in the middle of nowhere, being with him had felt effortless. Of course, she was also able to admit that she had used him as a distraction from everything she'd gone out there to escape. That wasn't exactly fair on him, was it? *But,* she reminded herself, *I did tell him that I wasn't looking for anything serious.*

Some part of her, the one conditioned by her stupid job and all the media she'd ever been subjected to in her lifetime, felt a little ashamed of her wanton behaviour. It was ridiculous, though. Why should she slut shame herself? If she'd been a man, nobody would think twice about her indulging in a night of no-strings-attached fun with another willing, very attractive person. She hadn't led anyone on. She hadn't hurt anyone. She did not have to suddenly fall into a relationship with this guy just because she'd slept with him and they actually got along well. And yet she still felt guilty. She blamed the patriarchy.

It was late. Overthinking it wasn't going to help. And her guilt was probably (definitely) misplaced. Still, her thoughts continued to swirl around in her head.

Hours later, Rosie closed her eyes. She was exhausted from fighting with herself. She couldn't control the pragmatic voices in her head that wanted her to stop being an idiot, but she also couldn't stifle the opposing voices of self-recrimination and doubt, either. She just had to accept the fact that she had made all the life decisions which had brought her to this point, and she needed to find a way to move forward and actually be happy.

A strange sense of calm filled her as she made this breakthrough.

Things weren't okay just yet, but they would be.

* * *

Rosie woke the next morning and felt much the same way as when she'd fallen asleep. Her feelings weren't as heightened as the previous night, but they still said the same thing: you don't need a man to feel safe and whole; you make your own world.

Rob was thankfully already out. She didn't want to see him. Here was the avoidance she'd been contemplating when she'd woken up beside him: the stereotypical 'run away from your one-night stand' bullshit she turned her nose up at whenever it happened in fiction. But this wasn't fiction, this was her reality and, as much as she and Rob had clicked, she knew she was a hot mess and it wouldn't be fair on either of them for her to get involved with him while she was working on sorting out her life.

Rosie very purposefully packed up her site over the course of the next hour, popped her gear into the boot of her car, cast one last look over her empty campsite and left. As soon as she got in her car she felt better. By the time she hit the highway, it was as if the trip had never happened.

She'd had a lot of time to think and to process the state of things on her drive back.

Rosie's family had been her whole early life. Sure, her mother vexed her, but Rosie did love her, even though she and her mother couldn't be in the same room together for too long. And her brother, for all her posturing, was her rock. She adored him. Her closest friends, Liv and Grant, weren't just friends. They were living memories of all the nights out, the dinners, and the laughs over the years.

She didn't need anyone else.

Chapter Seven

A couple of hours following her departure from the campsite, Rosie zoomed into her apartment's carpark feeling lighter than she had in months. She grabbed her handbag and headed upstairs, leaving all the camping gear to be dealt with another day. It felt good to be home. Refreshing, even.

Rosie slid the key into the lock of her apartment, turned it and pushed the door open. There was her brother, sitting on her couch with a bag of chips, looking for all the world like a cat caught eating cream. She couldn't even be mad. If she wasn't using her apartment, he might as well instead.

"You're home!" Micah observed with no small amount of incredulity. She smiled and gave him a big hug, and he practically choked.

"Ew, no!" he announced, pushing her off him.

Laughing, she took a step back in understanding. She stank like bug repellent, stale sweat and dirt, and the potent leaves of whatever tree she'd been camping nearby. She was a tad sunburned and kind of starving. The thought of a steak burger with the works made her salivate. But first, a shower!

Rosie left her brother to finish the episode of the show he was watching, set her phone on charge, and headed for the shower. Not ten minutes later, just as she was stepping out of a cosy cloud of steam, there was a knock on the front door.

Rosie wrapped a towel around herself and stepped out from the bathroom, signalling for her brother to get it. She shouldn't be home. Micah shouldn't be here. Why would anybody be knocking on her door?

She didn't have to wait long for her answer, given that her brother had bounded over to the door and opened it with the same excitement as a three-year-old or a puppy. Micah's eyes went wide, and he beamed a big smile.

"Livvy!" he called out gleefully, stretching the syllables into a childish greeting. Rosie groaned. She loved her bestie, she really did, but putting Liv and Micah together in a room usually spelled trouble for her.

"Hey," Rosie greeted with caution, "what are you doing here?" It was unlike Liv to just turn up unannounced.

But, considering Rose's phone had been flat thanks to the camping, she had no cause to doubt that Liv had tried. With advanced warning, Rosie normally ensured Micah - who adored Liv like a second sister - was far, far away.

"Don't 'hey' me!" Liv stomped forward, waggling her index finger accusingly. "You don't get to fall off the face of the planet for forty-eight hours and then act all innocent."

Rosie's phone buzzed where it was charging, still registering the missed calls and texts from the previous day. She picked it up and scrolled through. Liv had called, so points for that, but this situation was still not ideal.

Her brother chose to respond to Liv when Rosie didn't. "She ran away."

Rosie busied herself with her phone to avoid her friend's concerned glance as she asked, "Why?"

Proving he wasn't anywhere as astute as he thought he was, Micah shrugged. "Too many dicks on the dance floor, I guess."

"You're an idiot," Rosie huffed, keeping her eyes firmly on the notifications which were still loading.

Liv, on the other hand, cocked her head at him. "Is this about the relationships piece she's working on?" He nodded and she raised a hand, counting down on her fingers. "In the last twelve years there's been Jimmy, Sam, an extended break, Sam again because she's a sucker for punishment, and D."

Rosie could see Micah playing out the line-up in his head. It was almost as though she could read his thoughts about them. Micah hadn't really known about Jimmy. He hadn't met Sam the first time around, but had told her that he thought the guy had seemed like a flake when they'd met during Rose's second attempt at a relationship with him. And then there'd been Dumbass Damian. A total dick.

"Four chapters, or pieces of a puzzle, or parts of a map," Liv added, and for the first time ever Rosie rolled her eyes at her friend's attempts to be poetic.

"Your mother would be a big piece too," Liv continued to muse, almost to herself, "and you," she jerked her chin in Micah's direction, "and your father...and Grant...and me too, I guess."

"You realise I'm here in the room with you, right?" Rosie interrupted again, this time with a bit more vehemence. Her phone appeared to have finished loading her missed notifications, and a text from Margot stood out:

'If you want to keep your job, you will answer your goddamn phone!'

Something was wrong. The image of Nancy accidentally lighting the office on fire came into her mind, putting a stupid little smirk on Rosie's face. Still, it would be best to see what Margot's latest rant was all about.

She looked up from her phone to the image of Liv and Micah both waiting for her to continue to defend herself. It was almost comical. Rosie locked eyes with her friend, pretending Micah didn't exist, and explained the situation.

"Something's come up at work. I have to go in. Could be a while, might not be. You can stay here in the meantime. I have to get ready."

And then she turned around and got ready for a potentially rough meeting with all the confidence in the world.

At least she wouldn't have to sit through Micah's fanboying over her best friend, or have to deal with Liv's disappointment in her actions.

* * *

"Where the *hell* have you been?" Margot demanded the second Rosie crossed the threshold to her office. She was seated behind her desk, enough paperwork scattered across the usually pristine surface to have destroyed a small rainforest. The look on her face did not bode well at all for Rosie.

Smoothing down her pencil skirt, Rosie stepped further into the veritable lion's den and shut the door behind her. "I took leave. Technically, I'm still-"

"*Leave?*" The way her employer echoed the word made it sound like a curse. A perfectly shaped eyebrow winged upwards as she levelled Rosie with a stare. She sounded genuinely baffled when she asked, "Why?"

With an internal eyeroll, Rosie answered, "I needed a little personal time. I have plenty of leave saved up, so I thought why not?"

"I'll tell you why not! Because we needed you here!"

The younger woman stared back blankly. It was better than to ask any of the dry, borderline insulting questions about the necessity of their 'work'. She couldn't even think the word without the inverted commas. "I submitted at least a week's worth of extra content before I left." The 'don't tell me you've used it all' went unspoken but was heard between them anyway. Margot's eyes narrowed.

"There's specific content I need from you."

Rosie did not want to know. She wanted to turn around and enjoy the last few days of her rightfully earned time off in peace. Yet her feet somehow led Rosie in the opposite direction, forcing her to the seat in front of Margot's desk, while her mouth separated from her brain and prompted, "Oh?"

There was a definite expression of smug victory on her boss's face as the older woman leaned back in her chair and regarded Rosie over the fine gold rims of her glasses. "Your train-wreck social experiment pitch," she began, unaware that Rosie's heart sank at the very words. "I was at a networking gala the other evening and happened to mention it to a Life Coach friend of mine, who introduced me to a client of hers, who has just started up a new dating app."

Rosie smothered a sigh and allowed her boss to ramble on, even though she suspected she knew where this ramble was headed. Surprisingly, it didn't take the older woman long to finally get to the crux of the matter.

"...and then Jorge's brother, in charge of marketing, called me and suggested that they sponsor it as an ongoing once-a-week blog piece. They've offered me...er, I mean, *us*...a lot of money, Rosemary." Here, Margot leaned forward, grinning wickedly and steepling her fingers in a manner most reminiscent of *The Simpsons'* Monty Burns. "They enjoy your biting wit and think you'll be perfect for their brand, really playing up the 'unlucky in love' angle and using every week as an opportunity to remind our audience that dating could be easier using their app." She spread her hands apart with this proclamation and finished with actual honest-to-God spirit fingers to punctuate the announcement.

Flashbacks to the horrific not-date with Jimmy had Rosie blurting out a vehement "God, no."

Fuck that, she thought to herself, trying to will her body to get with the program and flee the office. *I'm out.* One article might have been entertaining. Even retelling the Jimmy debacle with as much humour as she could muster. But to continue to humiliate herself on a weekly basis to sell some new dating app? Absolutely not.

"Why not?" Margot's expression had turned waspish, as though she couldn't quite understand why Rosie wouldn't want to do such a thing. Hell, maybe she actually couldn't. "It's a lucrative contract for us, Rose."

"Can't Nancy do it?" She hadn't wanted to sound petulant, but unfortunately that was exactly how Rosie's query had come out.

Margot looked at her as though she was stupid. "Nancy is happily married with a thousand irksome children."

Three. Nancy had *three* children.

With a twist in her own expression, Rosie muttered, "I don't know that she's *that* happy…" but Margot ignored the aside.

"We're running the segment," the older woman insisted, smacking her fist on the glass desktop like a fleshy gavel. The impact upset the scattered papers and a few pens rattled in its wake. "I expect your first draft by this time next week."

Rosie bit back the complaint that she was still on leave, knowing it would be futile. At that moment, her phone buzzed in her pocket, and she fished it out since it seemed as though she'd been dismissed. With the barest nod of acknowledgement in Margot's direction, she pulled up the text from Rob, whose number she had saved the previous day, and read it on her way out the door.

'Should I be insulted that you packed up and left so soon?'

Heat suffused her cheeks. She honestly hadn't thought too much about how Rob might feel about her sudden disappearance from the camp site and now, with distance between them, she felt slightly guilty for not even shooting him a cursory text following her departure. She'd legitimately ghosted him. Not saying goodbye was kind of a dick move on her part; she was willing to acknowledge it as such.

'Sorry,' she typed back, her fingers hovering awkwardly over the little keyboard on her screen. She drew her lower lip between her teeth and worried it. *'Some shit with work came up & I bailed.'* It hadn't exactly happened in that order, but that was a technicality.

Oh, great. Sleep with a lawyer just once and you start thinking like one, she mused with a liberal dose of self-deprecation. Still, she pressed send on her reply anyway.

"What are you doing back here?" Grant's voice, laden with surprise and accusation, pulled her from her text conversation. She looked up to find him leaning against the wall with a bewildered look upon his face. "Aren't you supposed to be off finding yourself? It couldn't have happened that quickly."

With a face like thunder, reminded that her holiday plans had been cut short against her will, Rosie tilted her head in the direction of Margot's office. "Her majesty demanded my presence." She honestly didn't care if Margot heard her bitching. Her phone buzzed again but she ignored it in preference of venting at her favourite colleague. "You won't believe what she wants me to do."

Rosie explained the situation Margot put her in, but Grant couldn't put together the dots. "Isn't this what you wanted?" he asked as he guided her down the hall towards his cubicle. "The core of the project is much the same?"

Rosie huffed, folding her arms across her chest as she leaned against his desk. She couldn't believe Grant thought the two things were anything alike. "This is sleazy. I don't want to put my exes on blast, I want to explore relationships kind of intelligently."

Grant let out a chuckle, "That's an oxymoron, hun."

Rosie felt like she was pitching solar power to the owner of a coal mine. It was time to concede defeat. Sagging a little, she pointed a thumb over her shoulder. "I'm gonna get to work."

"...selling your soul for a dating website," he quipped, playfully determined to get the last word in, but apparently not capable of reading the room.

She sighed and looked up at her friend. "That hurt more than it should have," she informed him, aiming for light but coming off a touch pained. The smile she shot him was tight, to which he finally seemed to realise she wasn't playing along this time.

"Hey, you know I'm kidding, right?" he asked genuinely. "I'm sorry."

She shook herself and attempted a brighter smile for his benefit. "It's fine," she replied, but the issue continued to bother her as she made her way back to her desk.

Her funk-free bliss had lasted all of two days. No sooner did she return home that all hell broke loose again. It was as though a lightbulb had flickered to life above her head. It was the job. Her boss. This place. *This* was the source of her melancholy. Or at the very least, the trigger. How had she not realised any of this before?

She thought of the project that she had originally envisioned, rather than whatever Frankenstein's monster Margot had cooked up. And, if she was being totally honest, the thought of her brother and best friend waiting for her to get home gave her the confidence to do what she goddamn wanted to.

"Fuck this," she spat, gathering her things and making a beeline for the door.

Margot could suck it.

Grant's words, though she knew he'd been joking, niggled at the back of Rosie's thoughts as she stormed through the office. Selling her soul. That's what this felt like. Her heart ached.

When she'd first pitched the idea, it had been a flight of fancy. Something fun and quirky. However, it had rapidly become something else entirely - a catalyst that opened her eyes to all the drama and misery in her pathetic little life.

Even my supposedly randomised playlist is against me, she mused as '*I Wish I Could Go Back To College*' from *Avenue Q*, one of her favourite contemporary musicals, started to play through her earbuds. She pressed skip. The song didn't seem as comedic at that moment. Or maybe she was just projecting all over the place.

The next song was '*Never Give All The Heart*' from *Smash*. She growled in frustration and couldn't turn her music off quickly enough.

Rosie needed to stop this. Sitting about moping and feeling sorry for herself wasn't doing a damn thing to fix the problem. It was a terrifying prospect, but she realised that she had to start taking action and changing things. Nobody else was going to do it for her. Her choices had gotten her to where she was. She needed to begin making better choices.

Her phone buzzed as she stepped into the lift, startling her from her musings. She quickly realised that she hadn't replied to Rob's last message, from when it had buzzed during her conversation with Grant. Was there a protocol for replying to one-night stands? Particularly when you'd just ghosted them during the middle of an existential crisis?

The message that had just buzzed, though, wasn't another one from her random camping encounter. Instead, it was her brother.

'*Had to bounce. Left Livvy at your place.*'

Eyebrows arching, she typed back, '*You willingly left Liv alone? Why? That's OOC for you.*'

He sent back an eyeroll emoji and offered no further information.

"Lame," she muttered at her phone, then switched to Rob's last message.

'*No probs,*' his message read, followed by, '*Either way, it was fun. If you ever want to meet up, don't be a stranger.*'

Rosie stared at it in consternation. She'd felt empowered by their no-strings-attached night together, but now she just felt awkward. Was he signing up to be a booty call? Was that even a thing? How did other people do this? It was confusing and exhausting. Or maybe she just wasn't wired for it.

'*Yeah,*' she typed back, thumbs flying over the little keypad on her screen, '*it was fun.*' She hesitated, unwilling to make the same offer that he had. Instead, she settled on, *'Good luck being Uncle Rob.'*

Sending it ignited a flare of melancholy inside her. It felt like a goodbye. Rosie knew she had been the one to insist that she hadn't been looking for a relationship (and she hadn't) but Rob seemed like a good guy. A nice guy. And she was releasing him back into the wild for someone else to catch him. Someone not as complicated as she was.

"He probably wasn't even a lawyer," she muttered under her breath, realising she sounded like a crazy person. "Any money he actually *was* a serial killer." Not that it made any difference to how much she had enjoyed his company, but it seemed to hurt less to consider him a liar in some way, shape or form.

"You're talking to yourself again." Grant's voice caused her to jump. His grin was wide like the Cheshire Cat's when Rosie turned to find him lounging against the opposite wall of the lift. She'd been so distracted that she hadn't seen him when she'd walked in.

Still stinging from his earlier barbs, Rosie rolled her eyes. "Didn't you dismiss me earlier, your Highness?" She knew she was overreacting. He hadn't meant to hurt her feelings earlier, and she knew it. But, in her sour mood, she gave in to the urge to lash out.

"Hey," Grant held his hands up in the universal sign for surrender, "I come in peace."

It was a testament to how irritated she was that she didn't automatically turn his line into a dirty joke. Instead, she slid her phone into her pocket and jutted her chin up stubbornly to eye him. "How can I help you now?"

"Okay, so you might have forgotten, what with being out in the wilderness for a whole two nights-"

"Hang on, how'd you-"

He waved her interruption off, "-but we're friends, Weiss. So I'm doing what any good friend should do, and I'm checking in on you."

"And you just happened to be in the lift when I got here?" she questioned sceptically.

Grant chuckled, "I saw you storm away from your desk and I took a gamble."

"Right." Considering she'd only told her family that she was going camping, and that the last time Grant had behaved this way it was at her brother's behest, it wasn't too difficult to put the pieces together. She was going to strangle them both. "You can tell Micah I'm fine."

Because she was fine. Totally fine. Perfectly, irrevocably fine.

She hated the smug amusement which lifted his irritatingly perfect lips. "Uh huh. I've known you long enough to know that's not true, hun."

It took all her resolve to not scream back into his pretty face. Because he was right, and she hated it. "Well," her tone was brittle, "I'm glad you're an expert on my feelings, too."

Neither could recall a time where his playful banter hadn't been able to rein in her temper, so he frowned and turned uncharacteristically gentle. Moving into her space, Grant tentatively placed a hand on Rosie's shoulder. "This isn't just about Margot steam-rolling your project, is it?"

The lift announced its arrival on the ground floor with a *ding*.

"Of course it's not," Rosie huffed, straightening up and stepping out into the lobby. Grant followed her, rolling his wrist as he strode beside her, gesturing for her to extrapolate.

She stopped and stared him down for a moment, but he held strong until she exhaled. "It's that I have more or less realised that everything kind of sucks for me right now." She bit her lip, not loving the wave of emotion which washed over her as she made the admission. "And I get that there are people who are way worse off than me, so I have no real right to feel this way. And I have to work out how to fix it. I'm just a little overwhelmed trying to work out where to start."

"Firstly," he told her after taking the rambled confession in, "it's all relative. Yeah, there might be people worse off for whatever reason, but it doesn't invalidate the fact that you're unhappy with your lot in life."

With wide eyes, she found herself blinking at him. "Uh, who are you and what did you do with the real Grant?"

"Hardy-har-har," he responded with a roll of his eyes. "Very funny. I can be serious."

"By all means," she turned her hand palm up and swooped her arm across the space between them with a flourish, "continue."

His expression was momentarily bemused, but he carried on, "Secondly, really think about what's going to make you happiest. Changing jobs? Finding love? *Finally* telling your mother to stop being a meddling bi-"

"Too far," she cut him off, her dark, bushy eyebrows pulling into a scowl. "She's still my mum."

"I apologise," Grant said, but there was something in his gaze which told her he wasn't all that sorry. Slowly, his expression pulled into a moue of contrition, but his words belied his true feelings. "You've gotta admit, you let her make you feel so bad about yourself. I know she's family, Rose, but blood doesn't necessarily a healthy relationship make."

"I don't *let* her make me feel bad," Rosie rallied, but her attempt to defend herself was half-hearted at best. Her shoulders rose and fell in a sloppy shrug. "It's just easier to avoid the conflict. It's not like me clapping back is going to change anything. She's set in her ways."

"And her ways make you feel like shit. Constantly."

The response 'She just wants the best for me' was on the tip of Rosie's tongue before she realised that she sounded like the victim of gaslighting. *Could it be,* her inner voice supplied helpfully, *because you **are** the victim of gaslighting?*

Her mother didn't do it intentionally. Or, at least, Rosie didn't think she did. She just had such high hopes for her little girl, and Rosie had let her down and... *dear God,* she'd been gaslit. Great. One more crappy realisation to add to her list for the afternoon.

She should have stayed out in the pine forest with Rob. They could have built a life together out there, living off the grid. Just them and the trees and the fish and none of her insecurities and drama.

She shook her head, brushing that thought aside.

"They do," she finally acknowledged, feeling defeated and drained. "But telling her won't help."

"Okay," Grant nodded. "Then let's leave that for now. You're miserable here, yeah?" She bobbed her head. "Then you know what you have to do, right?"

"Job search." Rosie responded dutifully, if a little dully.

He grinned. "Job search," he affirmed, clapping his hands together once, punctuating the statement. "Daunting, but exciting."

The corners of her lips began to lift at his enthusiasm. "Exciting? Really?"

"Hell yeah." Grant leaned forward, eyes sparkling as he explained, "Putting yourself out there; chasing bigger, brighter things; getting all dressed up and talking about how awesome you are; and making them desperate to hire you - it's fun!"

A snort escaped her. Of *course* he'd see it that way, whereas she hated having to extol her supposed virtues to prospective employers on the off chance they might decide to offer her a position. "We're very different people, you and I."

It was now his turn to shrug. "Apply for a couple of jobs where you don't care too much about the outcome-"

"Isn't that wasting their time?"

He ploughed on, ignoring her interruption, "-and use the opportunity when you're interviewed to practice building confidence to sell yourself. Do it a couple of times and then when you're interviewed for a job you really want, you'll find it easier to convince them that you're the shit, which you are, and that they need you, which they do."

"I mean-" she attempted, but he cut her off, brightening with the building enthusiasm in his rant-slash-lecture.

"And, let's be honest, nowadays most publications are online, so you can work from home and video conference or whatever. Margot's way? It's dying out. You know, we should all leave." He looked around and then continued with a smirk, "Stage a coup or whatever."

"Whoa there, cowboy," she laughed and then, judging by how his eyes glimmered with mirth right back at her, guessed that making her laugh had been his intention. "I'm just having a 'woe is me' moment here. We don't need to rise up against the system or anything."

"And here I was planning a rousing rendition of *Do You Hear The People Sing*," Grant informed her, bringing his hand to his chest dramatically, "I'm very inspirational when I choose to be."

"You're something," she teased back, flicking his hip with the back of her hand as she added, "Jury's still out on what."

"Mean," he accused, but he swung one of his arms across her shoulders as they slowly walked towards the building's exit.

"You can tell my brother I'm okay now," she informed him, attempting to shoo him away. "You've made it all better."

Grant studied her for a moment, quite blatantly weighing the truth of her words. He let her go and stepped back after he seemed to have decided she wasn't just spinning a story to get him to back off.

"Just…think about looking for a new job, okay?" he said. Rosie nodded dutifully.

"Okay."

Chapter Eight

"Are we going to talk about it?" Liv asked when she and Rosie were both settled on the couch in Rosie's apartment the evening of Rosie's return, both nursing matching glasses of wine. "Your random escape out bush, I mean."

Rosie snorted. "Out bush," she repeated, shaking her head. "I went camping in the pine forest. I was, like, two hours away."

"That's out bush enough for me, and I thought you felt the same way." The redhead sipped at her beverage, before demanding, "So what the actual fuck, Rosie?"

Knowing she couldn't lie to her best friend, Rose bit her lip and admitted, "I couldn't deal, so I bailed, okay? I just wanted to be away from everything in my usual life. Not my finest moment, I know."

"Oh, Rose." Liv's expression softened, and Rosie averted her gaze, hating the pity radiated her way. "Why didn't you call? We could have done a spa weekend or something."

What part of 'I wanted to be away from everything in my usual life' had Liv not understood? Liv was included in that – a shining beacon of everything Rosie wished she had been able to achieve with her own life. Liv was a successful journalist, proud of her career and achievements. Happy with her lot in life. Rosie was so pleased for and proud of her, but also insanely jealous. Wasn't it safer to wallow in her own misery than lash out unfairly?

Staring into the bottom of her glass, Rosie eventually attempted the weak explanation, "I just wanted to be alone."

She could feel the weight of her friend's stare on her as her admission was assessed. Eventually, Liv sighed and quietly acknowledged, "Alright."

There was a tension between them now, and Rosie hated it.

"Look," Rosie began, in a tone that was possibly slightly more defensive than she'd have liked, "I'm sorry. I just…I sort of snapped, you know? And you're on this high in your career right now, and that's so awesome, and…and I just wish it was me." She angrily swiped at the tears now trickling down her cheeks. Liv made no move to interrupt her friend's unintentional rant. Rose's hands gestured wildly. "Micah gets this big break and is fucking off halfway across the world, you've got this huge story which is probably going to take you international, or blow up your career or whatever, and I just want to know when it'll be my turn." She drained the last of her wine, glared at the ceiling, and demanded, "When do I get *my* break?"

She was an atheist, so she had no idea to whom her frustrations were being directed, but blaming some greater power for her failings seemed far easier than acknowledging that she was the only person with the power to make changes to her life.

Liv shook her head and reached for Rosie, but she pulled away. She didn't need to be coddled. She'd just wanted some peace and quiet and time alone to sort out her thoughts.

"Well," the redhead tried to sound bright and playful in the face of her friend's meltdown but it sounded forced, "I'm seeing why the time off was necessary."

Rosie scoffed. "Yeah. Time off which I've had to cut short because my cunt of a boss-" She began, ignoring Liv's gasp and reprimand, despite usually agreeing that the word she'd just used was gross, "-wants me to degrade myself even more than usual for her stupid fucking website."

In the background, Lizzo's song *'Truth Hurts'* played through Rosie's Bluetooth speaker. Rosie nodded along, her mood leading her to soak in the empowering lyrics, while she performed some epic mental gymnastics to apply them to her personal situation. It didn't all apply, but she *was* being held back, and she needed something better. More exciting. Just…more.

And, sure, in her wine-soaked brain, Rosie might have been misinterpreting the lyrics for her purposes, but she didn't care. Lizzo was a queen, and she was the embodiment of loving one's self and putting one's self first.

Rosie wanted to feel just like that. Strong. Confident. Independent. Not taking anyone's shit. Her thoughts circled around again as her situation seemed to become clearer in her mind's eye, the song still blaring.

Margot was holding her back. And Margot did *not* deserve her.

Combined with her ever-increasing rage, the alcohol, and her prior conversation with Grant, Rosie's current musings all came together and led her to one glorious conclusion.

"In fact," she stood and wobbled a little, which was unsurprising as she'd rapidly consumed an excess of alcohol on an empty stomach, "I know *exactly* what I have to do."

Liv frowned, watching as Rosie made her way on unsteady legs to where her phone was charging on the kitchen bench. "What are you doing?"

Rosie unplugged her phone while she grinned maniacally. "I'm about to lay down some painful truths on my boss," she declared, dodging as Liv attempted to lunge for her phone. Rosie pressed dial on Margot's number and brought the phone to her ear, ignoring her friend's pleas for her to stop and wait until she was sober and in a better frame of mind before she did something monumentally stupid.

But it *wasn't* stupid. Without her inhibitions, Rosie was finally doing something for herself – for her mental health and for her own damn good. She deserved to be happy, didn't she?

"So, here's the thing, Margs," she said to her boss when she answered as the last refrains of Lizzo's song empowered her, "I am better than you. I'm better than your shitty website. I still have no fucking clue why we all need to work in an office to post clickbait bullshit, either. But none of that matters 'cos I quit. Tell Nancy to sell *her* soul for you. I am fucking done."

* * *

When Rosie woke the next morning, safely tucked up in her comfortable bed, she immediately noticed the paracetamol and bottle of water on her bedside table. "Liv, I could kiss you," she muttered, propping herself up against the headboard and reaching for both. Her mouth was fuzzy and gross, and her head pounded.

She tilted her head back as she downed the painkillers, then, as she set the bottle down again, she saw her phone. Vague recollections of the previous night began to form in her mind's eye, and a pit began to form in her stomach. "Shit," she hissed. Her words to Margot were far too sharp in her memory for how much wine she had consumed. "I didn't. I *didn't*. Fuck. Fucking *fuck*."

With a shaking hand, she reached for her phone.

Amongst a barrage of missed call notifications, there were messages from Grant and Micah, a voicemail from Margot which she wasn't looking forward to hearing, and a Facebook message from a name she didn't recognise. She read Micah's first.

'*Spoke to Liv. Call me as soon as you get this!*'

Biting her lip, Rosie deleted the message and moved to Grant's.

'*Mags called in a Code Red. Says u deserted. This 4 real?*'

She didn't respond to that, either. Nor did she react to his atrocious texting habits like she normally would.

"Oh my God." Tossing her phone to the side, she hyperventilated into her hands. "What the fuck have I done?"

With nobody else there to answer, the panic increased, tears forming in the corners of her eyes while her sinuses stung. She was such a failure, but this? This was a whole new level of epic fuckup, even for her. After ranting some very colourful things at Margot during her wine-induced meltdown, Rosie knew there was no amount of grovelling that could fix it and get her job back.

How the hell was she going to pay rent? There was zero way she was going to move back in with her parents. Maybe she could pawn some of her belongings to get by?

On the duvet beside her, her phone buzzed with another incoming message. Rosie wasn't sure she should look, but she picked it up anyway. It was another Facebook message from a name she didn't immediately recognise: Stefan

Grace. The name tickled something in the back of her memory, though, so she opened it.

Her eyes were drawn to the beginning of the message train, and she remembered it all with a jolt. Stefan Grace was Rosie's Year Ten crush. She'd been a bit buzzed when she'd originally messaged him – the very first contact she'd reached out to as part of her stupid experiment which had started the snowball effect ultimately leading to her becoming jobless. It had been well over a week since she'd sent her message, and he was only now replying? Was this some sort of karmic joke? It wasn't very funny.

'Hey,' his message began, *'I'm sorry it took me a while to reply. I didn't want to tell you right off the bat that I didn't remember you.'*

It sure felt like the universe was rubbing salt tons of salt into a wound. Rosie sighed and carried on reading.

'So I looked back at our class photos and found you. Took a few days to find them. But I do actually remember you. And I'm flattered. Genuinely. But you're not really my type.'

She eyed his shirtless profile picture again and sighed. His response, while it did hurt, was hardly a surprise. But she wasn't attracted to all men, so she couldn't expect all men to find her attractive, either.

The second message he'd sent seemed to show a sense of realisation that he might have been too blunt.

'Please don't take that the wrong way. I'm not a dick, I swear.'

Instead of being affronted, she snorted, and her fingers flew along the keys on her phone, typing her response which she sent before she could rethink it. *'I get it. And I'm sorry again for the awkward, random message. It was kind of a social experiment for an article I was writing for a job that, as of last night, I no longer have. And, if you'll believe it, yours was not the worst response I got. Winning all around today.'* She topped it off with a sarcastic 'thumbs up' emoji.

To her surprise, the ellipsis denoting that he was typing a reply popped up soon after.

'Do you have another job lined up?'

Her panic, which had been receding with the distraction of his messages, flared up again. *'I wish.'*

'How are you with admin shit?'

"What?" she asked aloud, frowning. She typed, 'What sort of admin shit?'

'Filing. Answering phones. Paying invoices. Record keeping. Reconciling bank accounts. That sort of stuff.'

Was he offering her a job? It sure seemed like it. 'I did a little temp work when I was at uni.' It seemed like a lifetime ago, but she didn't think she'd be too rusty.

'Well,' he typed back, 'I could use the help. Paid gig. Just until you find another writing job.'

Rosie stared at her phone screen. It couldn't be that easy, could it? While she considered the offer, another message came through.

'And I get that my farm's a few hours away from Brissie, so you can stay in one of the guest houses while you're working here.'

She hadn't even thought about where the job was, or what exactly it was he needed an administration assistant for. The offer of having her own cosy little guest house on a farm seemed almost too good to be true. Hadn't she wanted an escape from her reality? This offer seemed to be exactly what she needed and more.

'Where's your farm?' She responded, pretty much having already decided.

'Just a bit outside of Stanthorpe.'

Stanthorpe.

Apple country. Boutique vineyards. A picturesque little township with heritage listed buildings and a real 'Hallmark Romance' sort of vibe. Rosie fell a little more in love with the idea, and suddenly the drunken, spur-of-the-moment destruction of her career didn't seem quite as terrible anymore.

Grinning at her phone, she was well aware that agreeing was an act of desperation on her part. Part of her knew that she should be questioning Stefan's motivations a bit more deeply, but he had caught her at an opportune moment. He could very well be a serial killer, much as she had mused about Jimmy and about Rob but, at that point, she couldn't care less. He was offering her a lifeline and she was going to grab onto it with both hands.

With relief coursing through her veins, Rosie typed, 'When can I start?'

Chapter Nine

After a refreshing shower, it didn't take Rosie long to pack a suitcase with enough clothes to last a couple of weeks. She knew that she would have access to a washer and dryer out on Stefan's farm. She had also gathered up her laptop and charger, some toiletries, and nabbed her pillows from her bed. Her camping gear was still in her car, so she just dumped her extra stuff on top of it in her boot. She felt oddly excited and free as she went about her tasks.

Rosie still hadn't responded to Micah or Grant, but she wasn't in the mood to be talked out of this impulsive and potentially reckless decision. With the address for the farm plugged into Google Maps, she drove out of her building's car park and headed out of the city.

With every kilometre, the weight on her shoulders decreased. Rose felt lighter and more optimistic than she could ever recall feeling. She knew she was taking a chance and that she had no idea who Stefan was outside of the boy she'd had a crush on when she was fifteen, and that this could be a mistake of epic proportions. But she didn't care. For the first time ever, she was riding the wave of being completely selfish and acting with her own interests in mind.

It was an incredible feeling. Heady and addictive. Was this how Micah, who always acted in his own self-interests, felt all the time? If so, she was beginning to understand why he behaved as he did.

Just over three hours later, she turned onto the farm's gravel driveway. There was a huge sign with the farm's name on it, advertising that they were offering farm stay experiences in adorable little cottage-style cabins. The gravel crunched pleasantly under the tyres as Rosie drove the long path towards the main building – a gorgeous, clearly well renovated Queenslander, with a wraparound veranda and white accents.

Through her open window, Rosie breathed in the crisp, clean country air and felt invigorated. There was no sense of anxiety or unease. Just peace and excitement. *This* was the feeling she'd been searching for when she'd gone on her impromptu camping trip.

She parked her car up next to an old Hilux ute which had seen better days and climbed out of the driver's seat, stretching out her limbs and back while she took a proper look around at her surroundings.

There were sprawling crops of *something* off to one side of the property, and beyond them what appeared to be a small copse of fruit trees of some description. Considering the farm's location, she'd bet her meagre life savings on it being an apple orchard.

On the other side of the main house was a cobblestone path that led down past the rolling greenery where she could see sheep dotting the pastures and towards a line of cute little cabins. She figured that the cabins were the guest houses for the farm stay, as well as her home for the foreseeable future.

Rosie could hear chickens clucking away, though she couldn't see them, and assumed that they were cooped up somewhere behind the house.

"Made it safely, I see," a deep voice startled her from her musings. Rosie tilted her head back, raising a hand against the glare of the sun to find her new boss leaning against the veranda balustrade above her.

She grinned up at him. "Yeah, no problems." She gestured around her. "This place is incredible."

Brushing a lock of his blond hair out of his eyes, Stefan smiled back. "Thanks." He straightened and pushed himself off the balustrade and, turning to walk down the nearby front stairs, he said, "I'm pretty proud of it."

Rosie couldn't help sizing him up as he strode towards her. He wasn't much taller than her, but he was every bit as broad and muscular as his Facebook profile pic had led her to imagine. His smile was warm and genuine, and his eyes were friendly. "You should be," she replied, finding her voice again. "And, you know, thank you for offering me the job."

Nodding, Stefan made his way over to her car and popped the boot, grabbing her suitcase and tucking her pillows under his arm. "Thank you for accepting it," he answered, already setting off down the cobbled path. He spoke over his shoulder as Rosie trotted to keep up, "I'm hoping you can help get me out of a mess, to be honest. My partner was taking care of the paperwork and, after he fucked off, I kind of let it all get out of hand. My lawyer's gonna have my head, I reckon. And the accountant will have what's left."

"I'm sure it's not that bad," Rosie offered; to which Stefan scoffed.

"Mate, I'm good at operations and running the joint, but paperwork has never been my thing. I've got about a thousand emails with contract queries between me an' some of the businesses I supply produce to, and I haven't touched the Profit 'n Loss rec for the farm-stay side of the business in...*ugh*," he tilted his head from side to side, "three months?"

It was beginning to dawn on Rosie that she may have bitten off more than she could chew. "But you've got an accountant and contract lawyer, yeah? Because I'm good with the basics, but I wouldn't know where to start a Profit and Loss reconciliation or ledger or whatever. And I'm happy to look over contracts, but I have no idea about contract negotiations or anything."

"Oh, yeah, don't stress," he grinned. "Allen, my accountant, is damn good at his job, so as long as you can help fish out all the receipts and do a bit of a bank rec, you're gold. And RJ, my contract lawyer, will have all the other shit handled. He might just need you to dig up proof of delivery on orders and stuff, y'know? Show we're meeting our obligations, that sort of thing."

The stirrings of concern began to recede, and she found herself smiling back as they slowed their pace and came to stop outside the first little cabin in the row of eight. They were adorable, all timber and painted white, with individual picket fences around each one and with a good five or so metres separating each cabin from the next.

Rosie was instantly in love.

Stefan led her through the gate to her own little cottage and unlocked the door, handing her the key as he gestured for her to enter before him. She gasped as she took in the beautifully decorated space inside.

"This is gorgeous," she informed him, stepping forward to run her finger over the mantle of the fireplace against the far wall. It was springtime, so the weather was warming up, but she knew Stanthorpe often got frosty - especially in winter. Snuggling up in front of a roaring fire would be the perfect way to spend an evening.

Within the large open plan space, the fireplace was set across from a king-sized bed complete with lofty pillows and what looked to be a proper down comforter. On the other side of the generous space was a little country-style kitchenette complete with a dining table set for two. The windows in the kitchen/dining area looked out onto a vegetable patch. Between the kitchen and the bedroom/living space, directly across from the front door and on the opposite side of the main room was a door that led to the bathroom.

"Yeah, this is usually what we call the honeymoon suite," Stefan informed her. "The others have queen-sized beds and no bathtubs. This one's got a spa."

"Oh," Rosie swung back around, shaking her head, "I'm happy with one of the normal cabins. I'm sure this one is your most popular." It certainly sounded like the most romantic, which would be a waste on her single self.

"Nah. This one's all yours. I know being out here is going to be a big adjustment, and you've done me a huge favour dropping everything to come help out."

"Which you're paying me for and providing free accommodation. Besides, it wasn't like I had any other job to go to." The last sentence was muttered as an aside and, as the admission left her lips, she couldn't help but feel a little pathetic.

"Yeah…what happened there?" Stefan asked as he dropped her suitcase by the kitchen table and straddled one of the timber chairs, folding his arms on the back and resting his chin on top of them. "You said you were a writer?"

Rosie didn't want to go through the whole mess, but she had to give him something. She sighed and sat down heavily on the edge of the bed. "The job wasn't what I'd hoped it would be, and my boss was…well, she pushed my buttons, and I had a whole lot of other stuff going on and I…" She toyed with the soft material of the duvet, averting her gaze. "I snapped. I'd had a little too much wine and I called her and, *ugh*, let's just say there was no coming back from that."

He chuckled and shook his head. "You drunk dialled your boss? You've got balls, Rosie."

"That's one way to look at it," she shrugged, the corners of her own lips lifting. Her tone turned conspiratorial. "I mean, it did feel awesome and liberating." After another beat, where she recalled the panic and regret, she bit her lip and added, "But I honestly don't know what I would have done if you hadn't miraculously offered me a job."

"Well, the timing worked out for both of us." Stefan's response was spoken with a definitive air and he stood up, which seemed to punctuate the statement. "Wanna see the rest of the farm?"

Beaming, Rosie nodded.

* * *

The farm was beautiful. It was huge -fourteen hectares, Stefan informed Rosie proudly from the driver's seat of his ute- and amazingly maintained. Stefan had a few staff helping out with the operations, and Rosie had been introduced to them as she and Stefan did their rounds, but she had already forgotten their names.

Stefan had two large, white, fluffy dogs, which Rosie had thought were Great Pyrenees, but he had informed her were actually Maremma sheep dogs. They were friendly and well trained and helped to herd the sheep and cattle. Rosie was sad to leave them in the pastures so she could continue her tour of the property. She would have loved to have played with them longer.

They finished up at the main house where Stefan led her to the office. He'd warned her it was a mess, but she hadn't anticipated just how daunting the piles of paperwork scattered across the large corner desk would be until she saw the state of the room. The chaos spread everywhere, with a mixture of invoices, receipts and letters covering the desk's entire surface and even the computer's keyboard.

"Holy crap," Rosie observed as she stepped into the space, while Stefan hovered in the doorway, shamefaced.

He rubbed the back of his neck. "Yeah...I did tell you I was shit with this stuff."

There was no order to the spread of documents. Bills intermingled with invoices to clients and letters to and from business partners. This was the first time since she'd arrived that Rosie began to feel genuinely anxious. "This is..." she struggled to explain her concern that she wasn't qualified to fix a mess of this magnitude. Standing in front of the desk, she looked back towards the doorway in horror. "It's going to take a lot longer to sort out than I thought."

"Yeah," he nodded, his expression grave. After having spent hours watching him lit up and laughing, this change in him unsettled her. "I didn't think it'd be a quick fix," Stefan confirmed. "And it's my own fault, y'know? I just...I let it all fall to shit after Jase left. I wasn't in a great place."

It was the first time that Stefan had named his business partner. Rosie wondered if they'd had a falling out, rather than just parting ways. He seemed genuinely aggrieved, reminding her of how she'd felt after her breakup, and he clearly hated discussing the dissolution of his partnership. Not wanting to press the issue and upset him further, Rosie let it drop. Instead, she turned back to the daunting mess and set her jaw in determination. "Well, I'd better get cracking, then, hey?"

He brightened marginally but stayed in the doorway. "I'll, uh, leave you to it then. I'd offer to help, but..." he gestured to the mess he'd already made, "I'm responsible for *that*, so I reckon I'd do more harm than good."

"It's okay," Rosie replied. And it was. A baptism by fire would keep her mind off the mess she'd made of her own life. She shooed him off with a hand motion. "I'll start working it out. You go do whatever operational things you need to do. I've got your number-" they'd exchanged them during her tour of the property, when they'd stopped to eat a lunch of sandwiches and fruit from the portable fridge in the back of his ute, "-and I'll call if I have any questions." She imagined there'd be a lot of them.

"Thanks, Rosie." His shoulders sagged with obvious relief. "You're a life saver."

"Just returning the favour."

* * *

Rosie spent the entire afternoon and well into the evening sorting and filing documents. Unsure of the original system, she'd searched through the stack of lever arch files she had discovered in the cupboards lining the back wall of the office. Searching through them helped her to orientate herself with the way things had been working before. Jase (or Jason Crichton, as the paperwork had informed her) had been meticulous with his record keeping, making her life a lot easier. She'd even found a folder full of instructions and procedures to follow in his absence – clearly written for a time when he'd taken holidays and left the office in the hands of a temp.

"The hell are you still doing here?" Stefan's voice startled her. Rosie set the folder down on the desk, which she had finally cleared of clutter.

Rosie blinked up at him, her eyes suddenly realising how dark it had gotten. She'd switched the desk lamp on a little while earlier, but the rest of the room and the world outside the window to her left were almost pitch black. She glanced at her watch and startled. It was after seven o'clock. Her stomach rumbled. "Shit," she offered in response, "I hadn't realised the time."

Stefan reached for the actual light switch on the wall and flicked it on. The room became fully illuminated. Rosie squinted as her eyes tried to adjust to the change. Stefan took a cautious step inside and whistled. "Damn," he said appreciatively, "I hardly recognise the place."

Rosie had sorted, filed, tidied, and then wiped down all the dust and cobwebs that had accumulated. Weariness began to set in as the adrenaline from her focus faded away. "Yeah," she yawned, "it looks like an actual office again, right?"

"Right." He smiled but the tone of his voice seemed a little bit *off* to Rosie. Stefan stepped back into the doorway, tilting his neck in a gesture for her to join him. "Wanna have dinner with me? It's just a stew I made in the slow cooker, but all the produce is home grown."

Rosie's stomach rumbled again. "That sounds amazing."

He led her through the house. She quickly popped into the bathroom along the way, her bladder desperate for relief, and then made her way into the kitchen and dining area. The smell of the beef stew had Rosie's mouth watering as Stefan dished it up. Generous chunks of carrot, potato, celery and other vegetables, as well as thick pieces of beef, were accompanied by a thick, rich sauce. It was all she could do not to dig in before Stefan sat down beside her at the old timber table.

Flavours exploded in Rosie's mouth as she ate her first spoonful. She couldn't contain the moan of appreciation, blushing as soon as she realised the sound had come from her. "Sorry," she felt her cheeks burning, "it's just so good."

"Thanks," he smiled back at her, kind enough not to tease her for her inappropriate reaction, "it's nice to have someone around to appreciate it. Usually the dogs get the leftovers, and they're not really forthcoming with the compliments to the chef."

She laughed and shrugged. "I kind of survive on microwave meals for one, so anything home cooked is an improvement on that."

The scandalised expression on his face when she mentioned the frozen meals was worth the shame of the confession. "Well, I'm happy to keep on feeding you while you're here," he reached for one of the crusty bread rolls in the basket in front of them, splitting it open with his hands and dipping a chunk into the stew, "and I can even teach you a recipe or two if you'd like."

Rosie couldn't believe her luck. This whole situation seemed too good to be true. It was like she was being paid to take a holiday. A gorgeous private country cabin, free meals, and a job with a friendly, seemingly compassionate boss. At that point, even if this guy did turn out to be a serial killer, she figured her last days would at least be comfortable.

Reaching out, she grabbed a bread roll of her own. It was fresh and smelt amazing: clearly home baked. She smiled again. "I would love that."

* * *

Over the next few days, Rosie fell into a routine at the farm. She'd let herself into the office around nine o'clock and would work until lunchtime, when she'd stop and eat one of the sandwiches or wraps Stefan had made for her and left in the kitchen. Then she'd work until the evening, when he'd arrive outside the office and knock on the doorframe, and then they would eat dinner together just as they had on the first day.

Rosie had sent messages to Liv, Grant and Micah, assuring them she was alive and well, but gave vague answers outside of that. She was happy where she was, indulging in her selfish escape, and didn't need them to come knocking on her cabin door, insisting on dragging her back to a life she wasn't sure she wanted anymore.

Working in the farm's office was actually surprisingly enjoyable. She was picking up the ins and outs quickly, and had already become quite friendly with Stefan's accountant, Allen. Moreover, when she booted up the ancient computer on her fourth day, there was an email from the contract lawyer with some curly questions about a negotiation that had stalled between the farm and a large grocery chain.

Having spent a few days reading over some of the contracts, Rosie found she was able to locate the information for the lawyer fairly quickly. Rather than use the decrepit old scanner, she used the scan function in the notes app of her phone to copy the pages required and emailed them to herself before forwarding them on.

He hadn't included an email signature in his message, and though he signed off as 'RJ', Rosie didn't believe she had yet earned the right to refer to him by his nickname. After all, he didn't know her and hadn't actually given permission. So, she began a new email to roberto@owenslegal.com.au. After glancing once more at his email address, she typed out an email beginning with *'Hi Roberto'* and introduced herself as Rosemary, the new office manager, figuring using her proper first name was more professional. Finally, she attached the documents to the email and pressed send.

A reply came through a few minutes later thanking her. He'd signed off as

'Roberto' with a smiley face…directly above an email signature declaring his name was Robert Owens.

Despite her embarrassment, Rosie couldn't help but laugh that he'd playfully adopted the accidental moniker.

'I am so sorry, Robert,' she typed back in between giggles at her own gaffe, *'I just read your email address and assumed. Not enough caffeine for me this morning, I guess.'*

Another reply came through five minutes later while she was processing new invoices. It read: *'You gave me a good laugh, which is the best way to start any day. And it's a better nickname than 'Bob', I reckon. So, thank you, Rosemary. Have yourself a great day, too. Sincerely, Roberto.'*

She snickered again, and her smile stayed in place all the way through the morning and past lunch. When she recounted the story to Stefan that evening, he shared her amusement, his booming laugh echoing throughout the Queenslander.

"Yeah, RJ's the best," he said as his guffaws subsided. "He'd have found it hilarious."

"I mean, he seems to be running with it," she chuckled, twirling her fork in the mountain of spaghetti that Stefan had plopped onto her plate, "so he can't have been too offended."

"Nah. He's a really good guy, actually. Pretty down to earth, especially for a lawyer."

She bobbed her head, having also had similar thoughts about another lawyer recently. "Well, he seems nice from his emails, anyway."

The conversation moved on, and she forgot all about it until the next day, when Robert requested some delivery slips. He signed off his email as Roberto with a winking emoji, and Rosie found herself playing along. She sent her reply to *'Dear Roberto'* and closed off with a smiley face of her own.

When he replied with his appreciation and the words *'You've brightened my day'*, she cursed herself for the way her heart fluttered.

It was ridiculous. Sure, they were sending each other slightly flirtatious emails, but she knew nothing about him, except for his actual name and profession.

Still, Rosie couldn't prevent her reply in kind, and it wasn't long before they were sending casual emails with tidbits of personal information amongst the exchanges of paperwork. She learned that he loved chocolate, hated tea, and didn't have a preference of beer over wine or vice versa. In turn, she shared that she preferred savoury to sweet treats, had a mild coffee addiction, and *definitely* preferred wine to beer. They both loved dogs. She'd always thought of herself as more of an indoors-type...until she'd started working at the farm, of course, whereas he was an outdoorsman all the way, though confessed that wearing a nice suit and going out somewhere fancy was always kind of fun, too.

By the weekend, he had felt like an old friend, and she relished in their lightly flirtatious banter.

'TGIF! It's Friday night,' his email at four o'clock on Friday afternoon read. Robert followed this with the cheesy and ridiculous question, *'What are you wearing?'* He signed off, as usual, as Roberto with a winking emoji.

Snorting with amusement, Rosie typed back quickly, *'Only the sexiest pair of battered old jeans and a very flattering -if mildly stained- t-shirt and flanno combo.'*

His reply came back at quarter to five. *'Rrrow. Be still my beating heart.'*

She was still laughing softly to herself when Stefan turned up. "What's so funny?" he asked as she locked away the books with all the sensitive information.

"Your mate RJ is," she answered, then glanced at her watch. "You're early."

Leaning nonchalantly against the doorframe, Stefan tucked his hands into his pockets and shrugged. "It's Friday. I let everyone knock off early, myself included." He cocked his head to the side. "Feel like goin' out tonight? I can show you some of the town."

She glanced down at her outfit, exactly as she'd described it to *Roberto*, and back up at Stefan. "Give me half an hour to get changed?"

* * *

Stanthorpe was such a pretty little township. Rosie thought it was perfect and quaint, with its heritage listed buildings and scenic gardens. The Post Office was absolutely stunning, standing with its clock tower tall and proud in the middle of the main strip of shops. She almost felt transported to a different time, though she knew the insides of the buildings and stores had been modernised.

It was almost hard to believe that a place like that existed so close to Brisbane, especially when the atmosphere felt completely different. Where Brisbane City was all oppressive, greying buildings and hustle and bustle, Stanthorpe felt every bit a small country town, with smiling people and historical architecture and brightness and *life*.

Although Rosie realised that perhaps she was projecting yet again.

Stefan took Rosie to a local Italian restaurant. It was a little hole in the wall eatery; bright and warm, decorated in yellows and reds and had a homey, welcoming vibe. They sat at a table near the window, where they could watch the world pass them by. Rosie had learned a lot more about Stefan over the course of the week, but he was still somewhat cagey about the falling out with his partner. Considering she was reticent to talk about her own dramas, Rosie refused to push. If he wanted to talk about it, he would when he was ready.

"So, how's the first week gone? Boss not being too much of a dick, I hope," Stefan joked as they waited for their meals.

Setting down the glass of red wine she'd just taken a sip from, Rosie smiled and shook her head. "Honestly? It's been wonderful." She shrugged. "Who knew I'd enjoy admin work so much?"

To be fair, it was probably the escape from her actual life more than the job itself which had her feeling so relaxed and carefree, but she didn't want to bring the mood down by saying as much.

Her newfound friend and employer still eyed her knowingly. But instead of calling her on it, he merely flashed his white teeth at her in another grin. "I'm glad to hear it. You've really saved my bacon here, Rose. Literally."

She knew better than to mention the elusive Jase's immaculate notes. Reaching for her wine again, she brushed the compliment off, "I'm just glad to be able to help."

"Well, you've made it so I can hopefully finalise the contract with Woolies," he laboured the point by leaning back in his chair and staring her down with determination. "And that's nothing short of amazing, considering the mess I was in this time last week. RJ's probably gonna bring you a bottle of wine or chocolates or somethin' to express his gratitude for pulling me into line, too."

Rosie sat up straighter at the mention of RJ. Harmless email flirting was one thing but meeting the man in person was a whole different issue. "He's coming here?" Stefan nodded, midway through buttering one of the bread rolls from the basket between them. "When?"

"I'm thinkin' in the next week or so," he lifted and dropped a single shoulder in a half-shrug, still focused on his bread, " 'cos this contract is huge for the farm, y'know? He wants to go through it all in person. I'll probs be trapped in meetings for days." His final lament was punctuated by him tearing a bite from the bread roll more aggressively than was necessary.

The franchise in question was a grocery giant, so it didn't surprise her that the negotiations into the finer points of the contract would require additional time and attention. But it did surprise her that the contract lawyer was coming to the farm, rather than completing meetings by phone or video conferencing.

Expressing her surprise was met with another half shrug. "We go back a ways, RJ and me. He probably sees staying at the farm as a holiday, too."

"Too?" Rosie queried as she picked up a bread roll of her own, giving into the temptation the aroma had provided. It felt fresh and warm, and she suspected they were baked in-house.

Stefan pinned her with the same knowing stare as before. "Just like you do, right?"

Unable to argue with him and unwilling to respond, she popped some bread in her mouth and chewed.

Am I really that obvious?

Chapter Ten

When Rob had returned to the campsite after his fishing excursion, he wasn't exactly surprised to find Rosie's entire campsite empty and evacuated not even 24 hours after their night together. This did not stop Rob from messaging her.

He tucked his phone away into his pocket after his text exchange with Rosie and sat back in his reclining camp chair with contemplation. The whole thing with her had felt surreal. Like a daydream. This curvy goddess had seemingly materialised out of thin air, allowed him to enact an entire 'rescue the damsel in distress' fantasy, tasted like ambrosia on his lips, and had warmed his bed in a way that he finally realised he'd been desperately missing. And then she'd vanished as suddenly as she'd appeared.

Where some men might take offense to a woman leaving without so much as a goodbye, Rob didn't. He couldn't possibly. Rosie hadn't led him on. In fact, she'd been quite adamant about their fling being a no-strings-attached sort of deal. Yet, when she had hung out with him for the entire day after their night together, he had been pleasantly surprised. Then he'd come back to find her gone.

Something about the skittish woman had sparked life within him again. He thought of his promise to his sister. He'd told Belinda that he would put himself back out there again, give dating another go, and the concept wasn't as off-putting as it had been before meeting Rosie. Renewed interest stirred in his gut, and he resolved to see his promise to Lindy through when he returned home from camping.

Tinder, here I come.

Hopefully he would find someone on the app just as fascinating, flirtatious, and fun as Rosie had been.

* * *

"Well, look at you," Rob's personal assistant, Maeve, grinned up at him as he sauntered through the door on his first day back in the office.

Maeve was young, bright and bubbly. Rob had given her the job because she was not afraid to call him out when she thought he was being too demanding or not thinking things through. She doubled as the office receptionist, with her desk facing the wide glass entry doors, a few steps away from his private office.

"Looking well rested, Mister Owens. And very well tanned."

"Cheers, Maeve," he laughed. "Didn't burn the place down while I was gone, I see. Well done."

"Lose one fight with a toaster and it'll haunt you for life," she lamented exaggeratedly, pulling together a stack of folders and pushing herself to her feet. "Did you have a nice trip?"

"I did, thanks." He gestured for her to lead the way into his office. "Did I miss anything important?"

"Nothing notable." She sat down in one of the two chairs which faced his desk and crossed her long, slim legs while she quietly waited for him to shuck his jacket and make himself comfortable in his chair. She then placed the neat stack of folders on the polished, golden timber surface in front of her. "But David O'Hara called a few times."

Rob groaned and pinched the bridge of his nose. "If he's trying to rework the delay clause on the Collingworth contract again..."

"No, no, nothing like that." Maeve waved off his impending temper tantrum. "He didn't say exactly what he wanted, but it sounds like he needs a favour of some kind." She frowned, her blonde eyebrows pulling down with consternation. "I'm sorry I couldn't get him to be more specific."

"Secret Squirrel business is kind of his specialty, so don't sweat it." Rob reached for his laptop, lifted the screen, pressed the power button and waited for the system to boot up. "I'll let him know I'm back and that you are, as always, more than competent to assist him in my absence."

"I'm pretty sure he thinks I'm *just the receptionist*." Maeve made a huffing sound. "I could strangle that man sometimes."

Rob attempted to keep a straight expression. He honestly suspected that if he could get Dave and Maeve alone in a room together, they'd soon work out the tension which had been developing between them ever since their first meeting. And he would even endeavour not to tease them about their names rhyming.

"I'll set him straight," he said, logging into his emails and groaning at the mess which greeted him. "Why'd I take time off again?" He asked as he looked at Maeve with an uneasy expression, which soon became a feeling that travelled through his entire body.

"Because you were about to go postal otherwise?" Maeve offered. She slid the folders she'd placed on the desk earlier across the polished surface to him. "These are all awaiting your signature, by the way."

He glanced at the pile and bit back a sigh. "Yeah. Alright." His gaze flickered to the lower right-hand corner of his laptop screen while he fleetingly wondered what sort of joys his surprise camp fling was encountering at her day job, before shaking the thought from his head.

There was no sense wondering about someone he'd never see again, was there?

* * *

Belinda called him later in the afternoon. It honestly surprised him that she'd managed to hold off calling him until after lunch. Fiona was working magic on Lindy's restraint levels. "So, did camping relax you?"

Immediately, Rob's brain took him right back to lying in the afterglow of his encounter with Rosie. He'd felt boneless and sated, the very definition of relaxed. "Yeah," he answered, glad this was a voice call and not video. Lindy would immediately realise he'd gotten laid if she could see the expression on his face. "Just what the doctor ordered."

He could hear the relief in her voice. "Good," a smile sounded in her next words, "I'm really glad. I was getting worried."

Where he might have once felt irritation at the expression of her concern, Rob understood where his sister was coming from. Since their father's unexpected passing from a previously undetected heart condition, the two of them had become more than aware of their own mortality. They'd also endeavoured to be closer after having drifted apart some during their twenties. Where once they might have sent a cursory email or text every few weeks, they had made a habit of calling or dropping in on each other at least once a week. Lindy was the only family Rob had left, and he was all she had, too.

Sure, she was engaged to the beautiful Fiona, but it was wholly different to what she shared with her brother. And Rob appreciated that Belinda seemed to value their sibling relationship as much as he did.

"Well, worry no more," he responded with a grin, "because I am recharged and refreshed and ready to tackle anything."

There was a moment of stunned silence from the other end of the call. It occurred to him that he might have laid the enthusiasm on a little thick.

"Now, I know you like fishing, Rob, but..." she trailed off, then made a contemplative sound. "Did you join Tinder like you said you would? Because that kind of shift in attitude from you can only be explained by epic orgasms."

"How many times do I need to tell you I don't like thinking of the word 'orgasm' in any context that involves my big sister?"

"That's avoidance," she chuckled but refused to be distracted. Unfortunately, she was just as tenacious as he was. The very same qualities that made them both great lawyers also made her a pain in the arse as a sister. "So. Tinder?"

With a sigh of annoyance, he shook his head, though she couldn't see it. "No, I haven't joined Tinder. Or any other dating app."

"Huh." Lindy sounded a little flummoxed. He could envision her narrowing her eyes as she tried to catch him in whatever deception he'd tried to pull over her eyes. "But…you were still with someone."

She didn't bother posing it as a question.

"Lindy, I went camping alone." Once again, he was trying to deflect without lying.

"And you sound well rested and beyond pleased with yourself," she argued back. And then he imagined her waggling her index finger at him. "You're hiding something." After another moment, she whispered, "Please tell me you haven't started banging your secretary."

"What? No!" He was not that stupid. He needed Maeve's sharp mind to work for him, and mixing business with pleasure was a recipe for disaster. Besides, she was not his type. "Don't be stupid."

"You could just confess your secrets now, then," his sister informed him, unapologetic, "and I'll stop the guessing games."

"Or," Rob laughed, "I could say 'Goodbye, Belinda, I have work to do' and hang up."

"You're no fun."

"I love you, too."

* * *

"Mate, with Jase gone, I've been kind of screwed here."

Rob offered his friend-come-client an empathetic grimace over their Facetime call. It had only taken him a couple of hours to sort through his mess of emails and, after going over his calendar, had thought *'Fuck it'* and decided he should probably just arrange a farm visit with Stefan. Besides, with the Woolies contract still needing some work, he needed Stefan to pass along some supporting documentation.

"So you don't have access to the stuff I need?" Rob asked, his mind starting to whirr with backup plans and contract revisions.

Stefan shrugged. "I've just hired an old school friend to come help me out with the admin stuff, actually, so…give me a couple of days? She should be able to help."

The lawyer wanted to sigh with relief. He was already doing a lot of work for Stefan pro bono on account of their sisters being in a relationship. Having to overhaul the contracts would have been a major pain in the arse. "I can wait a few days."

"You're the best, RJ."

He couldn't help smiling. "Nah," he waved his friend's assertion aside, "I'm just trying to avoid doing extra work."

Stefan snorted. "Yeah, alright, fair call. Give it a couple of days and then email the admin address. She'll get right onto it if you tell her it's urgent."

He made a note in his calendar to do just that.

* * *

Rob laughed out loud when the new girl addressed him as *'Roberto'*. That was a new one!

After typing his reply, he blinked at the name at the bottom of her email. Rosemary Weiss. Immediately his thoughts shifted to the goddess he'd slept with in the pine forest. Was this some sort of sign from the universe? Sure, the name Rose or Rosie wasn't exactly uncommon, but to encounter another so soon seemed like a rather huge coincidence. Maybe even fate? It was almost laughable, except it just made him think of *her* again.

He picked up his phone and started typing a text to his camping fling which read *'Weirdest thing just happened!'* but, after a moment's consideration, deleted it and put his phone back down on his desk. Rosie had made it clear she wasn't interested in pursuing more with him, so continuing to text her seemed clingy on his part.

So why hadn't he joined Tinder like he'd promised Lindy that he would?

Though he didn't want to admit it, he knew he was afraid that any future dates he went on would be compared to the one who got away. The curvy vixen who couldn't build a tent but could suck cock like nobody's business.

And, besides how hot the sex had been, she had been so easy to talk to! She'd listened to his stories and had made him laugh and feel more at ease than he could ever recall feeling on a first date.

Not that they'd been on a date.

It had been purely friendly and platonic until she had kissed him.

But even when it had changed, she'd bantered with him, kept up with him in conversation, even when he cracked stupid jokes, and had felt so fucking good wrapped around his dick.

Then the fact that she hadn't been clingy or immediately launched into planning their future together had been refreshing.

Well, at least until she'd ghosted him.

Even though he couldn't possibly blame her, he could admit that her doing so might have bruised his ego just a tad.

And yet he still couldn't shake her from his thoughts.

Perhaps that was why he changed up his email response before he sent it to this new Rosemary and took on a flirtatious tone. Rob knew he needed to get over his attachment to a woman he'd never see again. Why not start off by following the neon sign the universe had just given him?

He wasn't disappointed when she flirted back. And if he imagined *his* Rosie whenever they exchanged emails? Well, that was his little secret.

* * *

"Your new girl's really entertaining," Rob told Stefan the next time they spoke, grinning as the other man laughed down the phone line.

"She is, yeah. And she's completely fixed my mess for me, so as far as I'm concerned, she's a keeper."

"Well, I gotta say I'm looking forward to meeting this miracle worker in person."

Stefan snorted. "You're only coming for the free room and board again, RJ. You can't help yourself."

"Admit it, mate, you miss me."

There was a heavy sigh down the line, but Rob could hear the smile in his friend's voice. "I put up with you for Fiona's sake."

"And having access to legal services on the cheap doesn't hurt either, yeah?" Rob propped his feet up on his desk, crossing them at the ankle. The legs of his pants rode up with the movement, proudly displaying his Loony Tunes themed socks. A gift from his sister. When Stefan didn't come back with a witty response, he nodded to himself. "Thought so."

"Like you weren't just confirming your plans to come and crash at the farm for a few days."

Ah, yes, that. "Honestly, we really do need to go over some of the new contracts in person. And it makes more sense for me to come to you. Especially with Jase gone."

Stefan's side of the call went silent. It wasn't a comfortable silence, either. Rob winced at the tension he'd caused.

"Sorry. That was a bit brutal." He paused. "How are you doin' with that? I mean honestly, Stef. You okay?"

It took another few moments, wherein Rob picked his phone up from his desk to check the call was still connected, before his friend replied. "I'm getting there. I can't say I don't miss him, but…" there was a loud exhale, "things between us had been shit for a while. It's probably for the best that he left when he did, 'cos God knows I didn't have it in me to kick him out."

"I'm still sorry, mate."

And he was. Watching any of his friends go through a rough patch was hard. Even if he'd thought that Jase had been using Stefan from the get-go, it hadn't been his place to say anything. Not when Stefan had seemed happy and settled. Hearing Stefan confess that things hadn't been quite as sunshiny as he had led on, though, made Rob wonder if maybe he should have had an earlier heart to heart with the man who would soon become family to him.

"It's fine," Stefan assured him, and he honestly did sound okay to Rob's ear. "Now that Rosie's here, I'm not stressin' about the business side of things as much, and it's nice having company again."

"Thinking of switching teams?" Rob teased, leaning back in his seat again. "Your Rosie sounds worth it."

There he went, fixating and daydreaming again. He couldn't help it.

In his mind's eye, Rob pictured riotous dark curls and deep, chocolate-coloured eyes; ample breasts and thick thighs; and a butt begging to be squeezed and held as he pounded into her.

He couldn't help that, either. It was simple word association. 'Rosie' would forever be associated with his voluptuous goddess. This was likely compounded by the fact that she was the last woman he'd been intimately acquainted with, and the first in a long time, besides.

Over the phone, his friend's chuckle shook him from his imaginings. "She's worth her weight in gold, yeah."

"That wasn't a 'no'." Rob wasn't jealous. He wasn't. Not at the hypothetical joking which he, himself, had started. That would be stupid.

Stefan snorted. "I like cock just as much as she does. It wouldn't work out."

Now it was Rob's turn to chuckle and ignore the odd sensation which felt like relief. There was no reason to be jealous, seeing as he'd never actually met the woman he was flirting with and, besides, he and Stefan had only been messing around. "We'll have to get you a hot stable boy or something, then."

"A stable boy? Really? Been getting into your *Mills & Boon* collection again?"

Rob snorted. "Yes, actually. Loving the ones with Fabio on the cover."

"Rockin' it old school. Nice."

Rob laughed at the amusement colouring Stefan's tone, then, following a glance at the time, attempted to get the conversation back on track. "Anyway, you're good for me to come out on Monday? I'm thinking I'll only need to stay a few days max."

"The cabin's yours for as long as you want it," the other man replied. "But…"

"But?" Rob prompted.

"I've given your usual cabin to Rosie for the foreseeable future." There was a note of apology in Stefan's voice. "It's the best one, y'know? And she did me a solid, comin' out here with zero warning. Least I could do was give her the room with the tub."

Once again, Rob was unable to prevent his mind from imagining *his* Rosie in the luxurious couples' retreat. It was a cosy little cabin designed specifically with romance in mind. All the little cabins had potbellied stoves, but the one mentioned had a proper fireplace and a larger, cushier bed, as well as a large ensuite bathroom complete with a spa tub fit for two, where the other cabins had little bathrooms containing a shower, basin and toilet each.

If the Rosie in question was anything like the one he'd met camping, he could definitely see her sinking into a deep, hot tub full of bubbles, a glass of sweet, bubbly wine within reach, her skin glistening from the water and the steam. Then he'd slip in behind her and- *no*. No. He needed to stop his train of thought. It wasn't healthy.

God, he needed to get a grip. His camping siren was long gone, and he felt even lonelier for having let her go, even if he did still have her number. She'd been upfront about her intentions from the start, though, and he genuinely had not anticipated feeling this way. He wasn't usually one to pine. But there'd been something about her. Something that had reinvigorated him.

"...earth to RJ?" The tinny sound of Stefan's voice had Rob shaking his head again.

"Sorry, mate. I got caught up in thought." That was a standard character trait for him, though it wasn't usually over thoughts of a woman. "I don't mind where I sleep. Even the main house is fine if the cabins are booked out. It'll only be a few nights."

"Nah. Slow season right now." Stefan dismissed him. "So I'll get your cabin ready and see you Monday, then?"

"Please."

Chapter Eleven

Rosie's phone blew up with phone calls over the weekend. Her brother wouldn't stop calling until she answered.

"Where the ever-loving fuck are you?" Micah demanded when she finally gave in and pressed the green answer button.

She found herself rolling her eyes, feeling much more empowered in her new surroundings where her family couldn't find her. This was probably a very unhealthy revelation to have, she knew, but she was great at avoidance and denial. "Hello to you, too, brother dearest."

"It's been a week, Rosemary. We all gave you time to sort your shit out and have your little tantrum, but it's time to come home now."

The outrage and defensiveness which once would have risen inside her were nowhere to be found. Instead, she scoffed, "When did you and Mum become one and the same? Has she finally achieved her dream of snuggling her precious baby boy so hard you've amalgamated into one disturbing person?"

Yeah, okay, that was harsh...so perhaps she still had some resentment issues to work through.

There was a moment of stunned silence before Micah tried a different approach. "Okay, I probably deserved that," he admitted. "I'm sorry. I'm just really worried about you. This...this is so out of character for you."

She'd been reclining upon her sinfully comfortable bed and attempting to read a book when he'd called. Sighing, Rosie flopped back against the pillow and stared up at the timber ceiling, asking, "What is? Actually putting myself and my needs first for once?"

"Yes!" Her brother responded and then suddenly seemed to realise what he'd admitted to, so he backtracked. "I mean-"

"So, here's the problem." Rosie felt tired again. And sad. "Why am I the only person not allowed to prioritise myself? Why can't I be selfish, Micah?"

In the ensuing silence, she imagined her brother was thinking through his plan of attack.

"Well?" she prompted.

He sighed. "You can be selfish, Rosie. I swear. But...I'm leaving in a couple of weeks and I wanna spend time with you before I go."

"Oh, alright," she replied with a liberal dose of sarcasm, "because it's inconvenient to you, I'll stop putting myself first for once."

"That's not what I-"

"It is," Rosie firmly interrupted.

"Come on, Rose!" Micah lost his temper again. "Everyone's worried sick. You just vanished. Not a word to anyone, ignoring our calls and messages... Liv's been beside herself, seeing as she was the last one to see you *alive*."

Despite the guilt she felt for worrying her best friend, Rosie snorted with irritation. "I'm not dead, Mike."

"Well, you could have been!"

He actually sounded concerned. Her guilt expanded to include him, too. She was suddenly reminded how it felt to be on the opposite side of someone's selfishness. Though she didn't regret taking the sudden, random job offer, she was beginning to feel bad for making the people who cared about her worry.

Feeling chastened, she offered a mild, "I'm sorry for worrying you," then, before Micah could jump on her change of attitude, Rosie added, "but I needed to get away. I'm working. I'm actually happy here. I'm fine."

"But *where* are you?" Micah dragged the word 'where' out. "Do you have any idea how difficult it's been keeping Mum from having you declared a missing person?"

A large part of Rosie relished in her brother finally experiencing what a nutjob their mother was. She didn't dare say as much to him, though. That was a small victory she was going to savour herself. "I'm surprised she even realised I was gone. Except, no," her tone flattened out, "she was expecting me to help pack your stuff for your 'magical, life changing journey' – I remember now."

Idly, she wondered if perhaps she hadn't run far enough away from home.

* * *

"Rosie, you busy?"

Stefan's voice startled Rosie from the task she had buried herself in, checking over an invoice the farm had received from a supplier. She glanced at the clock and frowned. It was only eleven o'clock on a Monday - Stefan was usually out doing his rounds through the farm by that point. She turned her attention to him. His broad frame was filling up most of the doorway.

"Sure," she answered, not bothering to disguise her curiosity.

His answering smile was warm. "RJ's just arrived and he's insisting on meeting you right now."

"Ah," Rosie nodded, having forgotten the lawyer would be visiting. Her lips quirked into a cheeky, teasing grin, entirely prepared to banter. "I'll admit, I'm looking forward to meeting the infamous Robert-*Oh-my-God*!" Her eyes widened with surprise as Stefan took a single step into the room and '*RJ*' became visible behind him.

'RJ' may have been clean shaven and wearing a suit, but she recognised him instantly.

"Now *this* is a pleasant surprise," Rob greeted as his own shock melted into visibly obvious pleasure. He stepped in closer, his grin turning into the same charmingly cocky one he'd worn when they'd met in the pine forest. He rested his hip against the side of her desk, practically purring, "Hello again, Rosie."

Stefan's attention swung between them. "You know each other?"

"Not really," Rosie answered, while simultaneously Rob said, "Intimately."

They gave each other pointed looks while Stefan snorted. "Ah. I see."

No, Rosie wanted to argue, *you don't see*. But, really, how could she refute the conclusion he'd probably jumped to? It wasn't as though she *hadn't* slept with the sharply dressed man in front of her.

Fuck, but Rob was hot.

She'd almost forgotten how insanely attractive he was. And that seemed ridiculous, because it had been *barely* over a week since her little camping adventure. But, with everything else that occurred over the intervening days, it seemed so much longer than that.

However, having him in front of her again brought back the camping trip in a flood of pleasant memories. She'd thought him ruggedly handsome with his scruff covered cheeks, but this clean-shaven Rob was sharper, his eyes that much brighter, and the dimple in his one cheek far more obvious. And the suit...*wow!* It appeared tailored to fit his frame (and it probably was), and it drove home the fact that he really had been a wolf in sheep's clothing when she'd met him. He seemed somehow taller, broader, and more authoritative. He was sin in a suit.

Awkward silence had descended.

"What are the chances, huh?" Rosie asked into the strange tension, shaking her head. "This is weird." She forced herself to meet Rob's eyes. "It's weird, right?"

"In all the best ways," he agreed, his expression just as boyish as when he'd leaned against a tree and laughed at her attempts to set up a tent. True to character, he winked at her. "I'd go as far as to say it's a sign."

"Please," she rolled her eyes, "that isn't a thing. It's a coincidence at best."

"You want to get into an existentialist debate with a lawyer?" His tone was as teasing and flirtatious as his emails had been. She found it kind of comforting. He wasn't a complete stranger anymore. "Or any debate, for that matter?"

Leaning back in her chair, she sized him up exaggeratedly. She knew exactly how to handle him...in more ways than one. "I'll take my chances."

Stefan chuckled and their moment was broken.

As he was directed back out the doorway, Rob called over his shoulder to say that they'd catch up later.

Was that excitement or anxiety she felt?

* * *

Rob joined Rosie and Stefan for dinner. With the additional guest, Stefan had gone all out and cooked a traditional roast meal. Thankfully, Rosie had been able to distract her employer from any conversations about her previous 'relationship' (and she used that term extremely loosely) with his friend-come-lawyer by complimenting Stefan on his cooking skills and then immediately segued that into a question of her own.

"So," she motioned between the two men with her fork, "how long have you known each other?"

"A few years now. RJ and I are actually almost brothers-in-law," Stefan answered with a shrug before reaching for his beer. "Our sisters are engaged to each other."

Rosie's answering smile was genuine. "Oh, that's fantastic! Congratulations to them!" She felt a minor pang of guilt that this was the first time in a while where she'd been happy for other people's joy without even a sliver of jealousy creeping in.

"Yeah, well, this one thinks it entitles him to mate's rates," Rob joked, gesturing towards Stefan with the neck of his beer bottle, "but he forgets I've got a business to run."

"Says the guy who rolled up in a brand spankin' new Toyota Land Cruiser with all the bells and whistles. What'd that set you back? Seventy-K?"

"Eighty," Rob corrected dismissively, "but that's not the point."

Stefan snorted, setting his fork down on his plate so he could point with his finger. "And you stay here for free whenever you want, eating my food, drinking my beer…"

Rob's grin was mischievous as he leaned back in his seat, utterly shameless. "I'm keeping you honest. Making sure you're upholding the standards you set out in your contracts."

"Uh huh." Incongruous with his words, their host shook his head as he smirked with amusement. "Sure. That checks out. You couldn't possibly do your job without visiting." Stefan's playful sarcasm was palpable. It reminded Rosie of the way she bantered with Micah.

"How'd this happen, anyway?" Rob asked, shaking Rosie from her musings. He was switching his gaze back and forth between her and Stefan. He landed back on her, and he cocked his head to the side. "I thought you said you were a writer?"

Ugh. She'd been dreading this moment. Rob already knew a lot of her issues because, when she'd told him, he'd been a random who she thought she'd never see again. Taking him further down her rabbit hole of inadequacy wasn't something she was looking forward to.

"I was," she answered slowly, looking down at her plate as she pushed a piece of roast carrot around with her fork, "but when I got back, my boss and I...well, we didn't see eye to eye and I guess I snapped, for lack of a better explanation." Rosie still felt silly for having drunkenly put her boss on blast, but she couldn't say she regretted it. Not when it had led her to Stefan's farm.

Rob seemed to read between the lines because he set his beer down and reached across the table, placing his hand over her wrist. His palm was warm against her skin. At Rob's touch, Rosie swallowed against a surge of unexpected emotion. "It was obvious you weren't happy there," his voice had lowered, and his tone was completely serious, "so I'm glad that you put yourself first."

Clearing her throat, she nodded. "I am, too."

Stefan chose that very moment to add his two cents' worth. "Me too," he agreed happily, seemingly oblivious to the moment developing between the pair, "especially because it brought Rosie here to fix the mess I'd made."

Moment gone, Rob removed his hand from Rosie's wrist and sat back in his seat once more. He tilted his head in Stefan's direction, asking, "How'd that come about?"

Cheeks burning, Rosie answered, "So, you know the project I was working on?"

Rob stared blankly back at her. She cringed.

"The one where I was contacting past crushes to document reactions and stuff?"

Realisation dawned in Rob's blue-grey eyes, followed rapidly by amusement. He pointed at his friend. "He was on that list?"

"Yeah," her shoulders slumped as mortification swept over her. "It was Grade Ten. We took English classes together. He was friendly, y'know? He never treated me like I was less than. And I thought he was cute." Rosie's cheeks burned at the admission. She cleared her throat and decided that was enough of an information dump about why she had reached out. "So, yeah, I'd messaged him." She opted to tell the rest of the story quickly, like ripping off a Band-Aid. "His reply came through after I quit. I told him about the article that was no longer happening and why, and he offered me the job." Raising her wine glass in salute to her new employer, she added, "Best decision I've made in a long time."

Rob raised his beer bottle and clinked it against her glass, smiling widely. "I'll drink to that!"

* * *

Rosie screamed.

And screamed.

And screamed.

She was certain she was about to die. In front of her, sitting right in the middle of the pristine white tiles of her bathroom, was the biggest *mother fucking* huntsman spider she had ever seen. It was about the size of her hand -*perhaps even bigger than a chihuahua*- and utterly terrifying with its plump furry body, and spindly, prickly legs.

Logically, she knew that it was harmless. Huntsmen were nonvenomous and kept a lot of other creepy crawlies away. However, it was intimidatingly huge, and she suffered from mild arachnophobia at the best of times.

As she caught her breath and attempted to calm down, she wondered what the hell she was supposed to do. The main house was too far away and calling Stefan to come rescue her when she knew he'd already be asleep didn't seem a viable option. Turning her back to try and find a can of bug spray also didn't work for her because a) she wanted to keep her eyes on the fuzzy little fucker at all times, and b) she didn't want to get any closer to it…which she'd need to do if she planned on spraying it to death. Also, killing it seemed cruel, even if it terrified her.

"Rose? Rosie, are you okay?" Rob's concerned voice came through the main cabin door, making her want to weep with relief.

She backed away from the bathroom -her eyes never leaving the eight-legged monster on the tiles- and, once her back bumped into the main door to the cabin, she blindly fumbled with the door handle at her back. "Help," she begged once she managed to unlock the door and stepped forward so Rob could swing it open, not caring how pathetic she sounded, *"please."*

Rob rushed inside, demanding to know what was wrong. With Rosie's eyes still determinedly glued to the spider, she pointed towards the open bathroom door. She was abstractly aware that her hand was shaking and that she might be crying a little as she babbled her explanation.

Okay, she admitted to herself, *maybe my arachnophobia is a little worse than 'mild'.*

Her knight in flannel armour gently sat her on the edge of the bed before striding determinedly through the ensuite door. Rosie squealed and flinched as Rob scooped the horrifically sized spider up with his bare hands and carried it outside. He returned a few moments later to assure her that her intruder had been relocated. It was only as she calmed down that Rosie clocked what he was wearing.

Loosely wrapped around him was a fuzzy pink bathrobe. Not even the sight of his bare chest beneath it could distract her from the unexpected piece of outerwear. She giggled, then clamped her hand over her mouth, trying to remind herself that colour and fashion truly had no gender, and she had zero right to judge his choice of attire. Especially after he'd saved her twice now.

He seemed to understand the source of her amusement, but only smirked back at her. "Stefan's idea of a joke," he explained. "My cabin currently looks like Barbie threw up in it."

"Hey," she responded, doing her best not to laugh, "no judgement. You do you."

He chuckled and sat down beside her, nudging her shoulder with his own. "You're sounding pretty cocky for someone who just begged for my help."

With a smile still tugging at her lips, she acknowledged his point with an incline of her head. "Thanks for that, by the way. I hate spiders."

"I couldn't tell."

She laughed. "Subtlety has never been my strong suit, I guess."

"Meh," he shrugged lightly, "subtlety's overrated."

While Rob shifted his weight to get comfortable, Rosie couldn't help but feel like there was a world of subtext in his casual statement. They were all alone, late at night, hidden away in the privacy of her cabin. The Honeymoon cabin. They were even sitting on the bed. Her heart began to beat a little faster.

"Rob-" she began, but he chose the same moment to speak.

"It was a nice surprise to see you again."

Her cheeks coloured. "Oh. Yeah. Uh, you as well."

His chuckle was rich and warm as he shook his head. "I don't really believe that. But thank you for sayin' it."

"No," she managed to reply with substantially more conviction, "I do mean it." Rosie sighed and looked up towards the ceiling as her cheeks continued to burn. "I'm sorry I took off without saying goodbye. I've never really done the whole 'one-night stand' thing before, so I wasn't sure on protocol or whatever."

"Hey." The warmth of his palm on her forearm startled her; she found herself looking him in the eye. His expression turned earnest. "I'll be honest, that was kinda' new to me, too. So, y'know, I'm sorry if my messages after came on strong."

"What? No, they were fine." She couldn't really remember them if she was being honest. Exhaling, she flopped back onto the mattress, aware of him stretching out beside her, his eyes practically burning into her soul as she continued to make her confession to the ceiling above them. "It's just...when I got home, everything went to shit. I'm not in a place in my life where I should be dragging anyone else into my mess." She turned her head back to face him and offered him a conciliatory smile. "It really is a case of 'it's not you, it's me' here."

Rob nodded. "Okay, I get it." And he sounded as though he genuinely did. "But," he added after another moment as a slow, cheeky grin lifted the edges of his lips, "if you're keen on something a shade more casual, I'd be up for it."

"In more ways than one, I'm sure." She had no idea where her brazen response had come from, but Rob threw back his head and laughed. Rosie couldn't help but think that the mirth in his expression only seemed to amplify how handsome he was.

"Somethin' like that, yeah," he agreed as his laughter abated. Then he reached for her hand, smoothing his thumb over her knuckles. "So, what do you reckon?"

Bad idea! Her brain screamed at her. She was already in far too deep with this one. Not only did she know from experience just how fantastic Rob was in bed, but their flirtatious emails already had her somewhat attached to him on a personal level. It wasn't fair to him when she wasn't in the right frame of mind to be starting a relationship.

But it's not a relationship. Just casual. He said so himself.

Could she do that, though? Did she actually have it in her to enjoy a casual fling and then walk away? She'd never tried before. She had never *wanted* to try before. Rosie worried that this was the wrong man to start with. He was too attractive, too flirtatious, and *well* out of her league.

But, for those same reasons, she'd kick herself if she let the chance saunter away.

Her mouth answered before her brain could stop it. "I'm in."

Rob's answering smile caused her breath to catch in her throat. He was far too attractive for his own good, or for hers. Then he closed the space between them, pressing his lips to hers in a kiss which was surprisingly sweet.

It was not the sort of kiss she would usually call 'casual'. It was too personal, even if it was chaste and gentle. Perhaps even because it was those things.

Breathing in, she caught a whiff of his cologne. It was masculine and spicy and familiar. The taste of his tongue was also familiar as it flickered tentatively against her closed lips, prompting her to part them. They fell into sync, already acquainted in the tilt of each other's heads and the way their tongues met and twisted together. Though Rosie missed the beard Rob had worn while camping, the prickle of a day's growth on otherwise smooth skin still pressed against her mouth and did not go unnoticed.

Rosie relaxed into the kiss and let Rob take the lead. He kept things slow and exploratory, making no move to rush whatever it was she had just agreed to. 'Casual', he'd said. Why had she thought it would mean something quick and dirty? Their one-night stand hadn't been anything like that.

Her hands bunched in the lapels of his fuzzy robe and another inappropriate giggle escaped from her throat as she remembered what he was wearing. He chuckled back into her mouth, but she had no idea if he was in on the joke, or just tickled by her burst of joy. She didn't think it mattered.

"I don't exactly have anything on me," Rob told her after another stretch of kissing. He had pulled away as the sensations morphed from languid to heated.

It took a moment too long for the growing fog in Rosie's head to clear enough to understand his meaning. She shrugged and offered him a reassuring smile, her inhibitions loosened by her arousal. Reaching down the now open front of his gown *-when on earth had she been so bold?-* she slipped her hand beneath the band of his boxer briefs and stroked his cock. "We can work around that."

Rosie had no idea what it was about this man which made her behave so audaciously, but the pleased expression on his face as his length thickened in her hand made her feel sexy and powerful and on top of the world.

"Yeah," he agreed, clearing his throat as his eyes darkened, "we definitely can."

Then he was shuffling their position until he could slip his hand down the front of her cotton pyjama pants, reminding her that he knew exactly how to work her body into a state with his talented fingers. He toyed with her clit while she reminded herself to continue stroking his dick.

And yet Rosie's actions came to a halt when he slid his fingers lower and inside her. She rocked her hips, her clit stimulated by the heel of his palm as she fucked his fingers. The pleasure built, twisting tightly deep in her belly.

Her breath came in pants as she leaned into the crook of his neck.

She was so close. Rosie could feel the tell-tale signs of her orgasm approaching. She clenched around his fingers, writhing and desperate to come. She could feel her face heating up with her usual sex-induced flush. She knew if she opened her eyes the skin on her chest would also be splotched with a matching pink colour.

Rob thrust his hips forward. The movement reminded Rosie that she still had her hand wrapped loosely around his cock, which was now leaking precum and throbbing against her palm. He groaned as Rosie tightened her hold and used his own fluids to lubricate her renewed, if slightly uncoordinated, fondling.

Then he kissed her.

Unlike the others they had shared during the course of the evening, this kiss was deeply intense. Rob held nothing back, moving his mouth against Rosie's in a way which left nothing to her imagination. He kissed her in proxy of being able to make love to her, and this was all it took to finally push her over the edge. While his breath mingled with hers, Rosie mewled into his mouth as the blissful release of her orgasm overtook her. She was so overcome by the waves of pleasure that she was barely aware of him cursing and spilling over her fist in response.

In the afterglow, they lay boneless and sated, catching their breaths. The soporific effect of her orgasm had her snuggling against him, heedless of the wet spot beside her, or the promise she had made to keep things casual. Her eyelids were heavy, and his presence was warm and soothing.

"Stay?" she asked him, allowing her eyes to slide shut.

Rob chuckled, the sound vibrating through his chest. She allowed it to lull her all the way to sleep, missing his actual answer.

Chapter Twelve

'Casual' was a mistake. Rosie could see that now. Rob had extended his three-day stay into a week, and the flirting had turned into stolen kisses in hallways and long nights spent thoroughly exploring each other's bodies. It felt a lot more like a relationship than she was comfortable with.

Rob was *perfection*. He was the sort of man she could easily see herself falling in love with. But she wasn't in the right frame of mind to barrel headfirst into another relationship, and it didn't seem at all fair to him if she brought along all her unresolved baggage.

She had tried to warn him, so she didn't think his frustration was warranted when, on his actual last night at the farm, she told him that she couldn't go through with their casual arrangement any longer.

Rob seemed hurt by her declaration, steeling his once again scruffy jaw. He nodded curtly while she tried to explain. "It's fine, Rose," he said in a tone that suggested he felt otherwise, "casual's not supposed to feel like a chore."

"I never said it felt like-"

"It doesn't matter." He cut her off, shaking his head. "It's done. Easy."

It didn't feel easy. It felt like a breakup. She didn't like that at all. "I'm sorry," she apologised again, having already done so at least five times during the conversation, "I told you, I suck at all of this." She waved her hand between them. "I'm a hot mess right now. You deserve better than that."

Better than me.

His grey-blue eyes turned sad and he sighed, pushing himself up from his seat at the little table to look down on her while he slipped his shoulders back into his previously discarded denim jacket. "You don't get to decide what I deserve, you know."

Biting back the urge to apologise again, she nodded. "I know. But things are still so fucked up for me right now."

He knew all about that, too. He knew she was dodging her brother's calls and that she had even sent her best friend to voicemail twice during the past week. He knew she would have to head back to Brisbane and face her family and the mistakes she'd made with her career. He knew that she had no idea what she honestly wanted to do with her life, and that she wasn't even sure where she was going to live or how long she would be putting down roots when she did settle.

She felt bereft within her own skin. As much as she enjoyed Rob's company, and as attractive and perfect as Rosie found him, using him as a distraction from fixing the mess she'd made of her life wasn't fair on either of them.

Licking her lips, she attempted a peace offering. "Friends? And, y'know, if you're still single when I finally get my shit together…maybe something more?" Her voice pitched higher with hope. "Maybe?"

Rob observed her for a moment before his expression smoothed out into a softer, warmer one. With understanding in his gaze, he nodded and extended his hand for her to shake, "I'll hold you to that, Rosie."

Relieved, she shook his hand as though it was a business transaction. "Deal." Cheekily, she added, "Pleasure working with you, Roberto."

His responding laughter melted away whatever tension remained. She was relieved that she hadn't completely fucked things up with him.

Maybe she really was beginning to make the right choices now.

God, she hoped she was.

* * *

Rosie's luck ran out two days later when the barking of the dogs and the sound of tyres on gravel heralded an unexpected visitor to the farm. Seated at her desk, she looked up when Stefan knocked at the open doorway to the office. He was frowning at her with concern.

"Someone's here to see you," he said as she furrowed her brow back at him in response.

"Who?"

Before her boss-come-friend could answer, her brother pushed past him. "Me."

Fuck it all.

Micah glowered down at her, his arms folded and his face set with grim determination. Rosie sat back in her chair and sighed. "Looks like you found me."

"Is that *seriously* all you have to say for yourself?" He demanded.

"I'm just gonna leave you guys to it." Stefan backed away. Rosie wanted to call him back, to beg for his support. But he still had work to do, and this was a mess she had created for herself. She felt a pang of guilt for having brought it to his doorstep.

"Well?" Micah prompted, sounding just like their mother.

Honestly, she didn't even care how he'd managed to locate her. He'd probably hacked her Facebook and read her messages, because that seemed very much the sort of invasive, boundary-free behaviour he would indulge in. Or maybe he'd used his Find My Friend app or something. It honestly didn't matter.

"You couldn't have called first?" Rosie asked him, turning back to her computer dismissively. If this was going to be a game of who could out-frost the other, she thought she had a fair chance at winning.

Her brother's hand slammed down on the desk beside her. "You weren't answering any of our calls."

Alright, she had to concede it was a fair point. *Damn it.* Unwilling to give in, though, she continued typing the reply she'd been formulating to one of the farm's contractors. "So maybe," she responded with her eyes glued determinedly to the screen, "I wasn't ready to talk."

"Too bad," Micah snapped back, grabbing the back of her chair and forcibly spinning her away from the computer. "I'm leaving the country in just under three weeks, and Bren's wedding is in two." He levelled her with another glare. Admittedly, Rosie did feel marginally guilty for forgetting about her friend's big day. "I RSVPed for you, by the way. Back when you tried to get out of it. You can take Grant as your date. I'm bringing Liv."

Rosie blinked at him, stunned. He truly had morphed into their mother. RSVPing for her? Deciding that she was taking a date *and* telling her who she was taking? Who the *hell* did he think he was?

"And if I have another date lined up?" The challenge left her lips before she could properly think it through. She cringed as his eyes narrowed at her.

"Like who?" Micah demanded. His disbelief stung her. He gestured vaguely towards the rest of the house. "Steve?"

She didn't like the amusement that coloured his tone as he misspoke her friend's name. Whether it was deliberate or not, she didn't care.

"Stefan," she corrected, "and no." This was accompanied by a scowl as she folded her arms across her chest. "Not anyone you've met, in fact."

Obviously, her thoughts turned to Rob.

Rob, whom she had just navigated back to the realm of friendship only. Rob, whom she had promised to keep free of the mess that was her current personal life. Rob, who she'd hoped would once again bail her out of a jam. She'd owe him big time if he agreed.

Micah arched an eyebrow. "Your social circle isn't exactly huge, Rose."

His commentary hurt. For someone attempting to woo her back into her old life, her brother was doing a shitty job of it.

Refusing to back down or cry, she rolled her eyes. "Fuck you."

He heaved a dramatic sigh. "Just admit you're being stubborn for the sake of it," he urged, then made a show of checking his watch. Glancing around the office with distaste, he added, "Then pack your stuff so we can get out of here."

"*Excuse* me?" Rosie leaned back in her chair, widening the stance of her legs, attempting to plant herself in place. "I'm not going anywhere with you today, Mike. Or this week, even." She wasn't going to leave Stefan in the lurch. Not when he'd been so kind as to rescue her from joblessness and revive her sense of purpose. "I'll go to Brennan's wedding, and I'll sort out my own date, thanks, but I've got work to finish here."

With wide blue eyes, Micah stared back at her. His mouth worked, but no sound came out. He wasn't used to her actually denying him, especially not in person. She could tell he had no idea how to react. "Rosie, please." He'd shifted tact. "I miss you. I want to spend time with you before I leave."

She wanted to believe him, she genuinely did. However, he'd been attempting a number of their mother's tactics and guilt had always been her primary weapon of choice. "I'll head back next weekend for the wedding," she repeated firmly. "You'll survive without me, I'm sure."

"Are you serious?"

Turning, Rosie found herself facing a version of her brother she wasn't sure she had seen before. His expression was one of wounded disbelief, his eyes glinting with frustration as he stared her down.

"I'm working here, Micah," she reminded him softly, "and you didn't take any of my feelings into consideration when you decided you were moving overseas. How is this really any different?"

Something close to anger flashed across his face. "I'm moving to pursue my dreams," he shot back, then gestured vaguely around him, "and you're here because you ran away from yours."

"You think working for a fucking clickbait site was my dream?"

He shrugged. "It was a hell of a lot closer than doing…whatever the hell it is you're doing now."

Rosie worked her jaw, rolling her eyes towards the ceiling. "Because you've put so much effort into finding out exactly what it is I do here, right? Or what my dreams actually are?"

"Oh, *come on*, Rosemary. You want to write! You've wanted to write since you learned how!" He flung his hands back into the air and paced the small office space. "And I know Margot's stupid blog wasn't quite how you wanted to do it, but you could at least make connections there. I doubt you're getting any of that here."

It sucked that she couldn't deny he'd made a valid point, but she hadn't felt the desire or drive to write a word since she'd arrived on the farm. Didn't that also tell her something? Maybe the break was warranted? Maybe she needed to recalibrate and really think about her next steps?

It would be useless to try and explain that to her brother, though.

Instead, she allowed her shoulders to slump. Rosie licked her lips as she considered how best to respond. Eventually she sighed and said, "I don't want it right now. I can't..." Her throat tightened, and she paused for a moment as she composed herself. "Micah, I'm burned out. I honestly don't know what I want anymore, but I do know being here is helping." And, alright, she'd concede that a week of sleeping with Rob had probably had a lot to do with her much more mellow state. She stared up at Micah with wide, imploring eyes. "Please just trust me to work my own shit out right now."

Micah was silent, his expression giving none of his thoughts away. Eventually he shook his head and took a step back. "Fine," he folded his arms across his chest, "but remember – you have to deal with Mum when all of this is said and done."

Somehow, she didn't think their mother was going to accept Rosie's decisions anywhere near as easily as her brother just had. Still, his acceptance eased something within her. She pushed out of her chair and startled him by enveloping him in a hug. "Thanks, Mike."

* * *

Stefan gave Rosie a huge hug when she finally left the farm a week later. He told her, in no uncertain terms, that if she ever wanted to come back to simply turn up. There would always be a room available for her.

The words warmed her in ways she couldn't quite explain.

Micah, Liv and Grant were all waiting for her in her apartment when she returned home. It was good to see her friends again, but she steeled herself for their lectures. So Rosie was pleasantly surprised and relieved when all they did was wrap her in their arms and remind her that she didn't have to deal with her dramas and stress on her own.

Grant also cracked a couple of dirty jokes, but she could tell that even he seemed rattled at how abruptly she had left.

Sitting in her tiny living room, squished up between Grant and Micah on her couch, Rosie glanced around the apartment and tried to dismiss the feeling of wrongness being inside the space evoked now. She'd only been gone a few weeks, but it already felt like a stranger's home. She longed for the farm, for her little cottage and the sense of purpose she had felt from being able to actually help an old schoolmate.

And Rob, her mind traitorously added. *Admit it; you want him, too.*

When she'd called him and begged - literally begged - him to be her platonic date to Brennan's wedding, they had both acknowledged that it would feel awkward, even if they were trying to be 'just friends'. He made no secret of wanting to pursue some sort of relationship with her, even if just 'casual', and she was quite tempted to give in. However, until she sorted out her dramas, she knew it would be a bad idea and she told him so. Despite all of that, Rob *did* agree to be her date anyway.

God, she hated her conscience.

"So, tell us all about this mystery date of yours," Grant nudged her with his shoulder; she wondered if he'd become a mind reader. "He's got to be something special if you're choosing him over me."

"He's a friend," Rosie stuck with the same story she'd told her brother, trying not to squirm under all of their combined gazes.

Grant affected offence. His hand clutched at imaginary pearls beneath his neck. "And what am I?"

"Trouble," she answered, squealing when he tickled her ribs in response to her teasing.

Liv was frowning at Rosie from the armchair to their right. She still hadn't really forgiven Rosie for taking off again, that much was obvious. Steepling her fingers in front of her, she rebuked, "Except you've never mentioned this guy before. He's legit just come out of nowhere."

"I met him while I was camping." There was no point lying about it. Not when Liv would likely interrogate Rob when they met at the wedding.

Her friend's eyes widened. "Like…a week ago?"

"It's closer to a month, now," Rosie shrugged.

Grant chuckled. "He's a hottie, huh?"

"Mmm." She tried not to be too enthusiastic with her response. "Yeah.

But...we just clicked, you know?"

"Enough for you to choose him over me, though?" Grant smirked at her. "You want to jump his bones."

Her cheeks burned. She wasn't going to admit she already had. Numerous times.

Grant was chortling now. "You *do*! Oh, Rosemary, this is fantastic!"

"It is?" She asked, bewildered.

At her other side, Micah, sounding unimpressed, repeated her very question.

Grant nodded with enthusiasm, gesturing wildly with his hands. "You're getting over Dipshit. *Finally!*"

"I've been over Damian for ages."

"Eh. I think he's been lurking in your head for a while." Grant's expression quickly turned serious and a frown tugged down his dark eyebrows. "Made you second guess your worth."

"A lot of things did that," she acknowledged as she listed some off in her head. *Damian. Margot. Mum.*

"Yeah, well, I'm glad you're working through it." Her friend's arm wrapped around her shoulders and he squeezed her tight. "And if running away and joining a circus-"

"Farm," she corrected.

"Circus," he repeated determinedly, "was what got you seeing sense? I'm all for it, babe." He shot Liv a look as if daring her to argue with him. Clearly, there was still a bone of contention between them, and this whole situation hadn't made it any better.

"Thanks, Grant." Rosie leaned her head against his shoulder, breathing in the calming scent of his sweet and mellow aftershave. "I'm still sorry I asked him to be my plus one."

"Well, y'know, I am a little miffed that I won't be able to chase after any eligible bridesmaids... groomsmaids?" He cocked his head as he considered the terminology, then moved on. "Or groomsmen. They're usually easy pickings at weddings."

She smacked his chest. "You're incorrigible."

But his antics had achieved what being back in her apartment had not: she was comfortable and happy again.

The conversation flowed on from there, and she let her mind drift, feeling as though everything might actually work out in the end.

* * *

"I can't believe you let me think you'd been kidnapped!" Rosie's mother's high pitched voice greeted her as Micah practically dragged her into their parents' house.

"Meredith, you're being a touch dramatic." At least her dad had her back, though this only made her feel guiltier for not reaching out to him when she'd taken off to Stanthorpe. He would have understood. Hell, he would have even supported her.

She allowed herself to be pulled into her father's embrace. "Hey, Dad. I'm sorry, I-"

"What's done is done," he cut her off, calm and reassuring as ever. "I'm just glad to see you."

Her mother continued squawking. "She *knew* her brother needed her! Not to mention quitting her job and running away like...like an errant teenager! How humiliating!"

"I needed a break," Rosie couldn't keep her mouth shut, even though she knew she'd only be poking the bear. "I was barely keeping it all together, and-"

"Oh, please." Brushing past her with her nose in the air, Meredith led the way down the tiled hallway to the formal living room, which was carpeted in beige. Inside, the room was decorated with antique timber furniture in dark oak tones, which gave off a dated, cold, old money sort of vibe. Rosie hated this room. She sat heavily on the tan coloured couch as her mother picked up speed and volume. "What did you have to *keep together*, Rosemary? Hmm? Not a relationship, because you can't hold down one of those, and not a real job, because you refused to do any real studying..."

Rosie closed her eyes and let the wave of diatribe wash over her. All she had to do was grit her teeth, agree with her mother, apologise and then escape. Four *little* steps. She could do this.

There was a buzzing in her ears, though, and her heart was jackhammering inside her chest.

She recalled how good it had felt to put herself first, to make her own choices and to live freely. The feeling had been addictive, and now it was pumping through her veins, building a sense of rage along with it.

She could hear her dad and brother interjecting into her mother's rant, though the words were indistinguishable through the cacophony.

In her lap, Rosie's hands clenched tightly into fists. The buzzing in her ears increased in volume.

"…what am I going to tell the neighbours?"

The absurd question broke through the fog in Rosie's brain and a bubble of inappropriate laughter burst past her lips, as did the near-vicious "To mind their own fucking business, perhaps?" she couldn't reel back in.

In front of her, her mother's jaw dropped. Seated in the two armchairs positioned kitty-corner to either side of the couch, her brother's and dad's did the same. Silence descended.

"I beg your pardon?!"

"I'm twenty-eight." Rosie's hands were shaking but her voice was firm as she glared up at the matriarch of her family, feeling years of bubbling, festering resentment finally breaking free. "And what I do with my life is of no concern to the fucking neighbours."

"Language!" Her mother sounded scandalised. It was ridiculous.

"Twenty-eight," Rosie repeated, shaking her head. "I can say 'fuck' if I want to. I can say 'shit', too. And 'cunt' if I *really* feel like it."

Micah squeaked, and out of the corner of her eye she watched him attempt to become one with the backing of his armchair. She didn't dare look in her father's direction.

Her mother's gaze narrowed and she took a step towards the couch. "How dare-"

"No." Rosie stood up. The same burst of adrenaline which had seen her quitting her job motivated her to defend herself against her mother. "How dare *you*?" Tears gathered in the corners of her eyes, but she forged on. "My whole life, nothing has *ever* been good enough for you. Micah's this...this saint who you had no qualms supporting in his dreams to be an actor - arguably an even more competitive career than writing - and you never once pressured him to get a 'real job', or find a 'respectable' spouse, or settle down, or any of it!"

The words weren't stopping. A lifetime of repressed resentment had burst forth from its confines and was spewing forth with vitriol. Rosie knew this was going to destroy the remaining vestiges of pleasantry between her mother and herself, but with every grievance she aired, her shoulders felt lighter.

The tears trickled down her cheeks steadily as she continued. She counted her arguments on her fingers, "You never make him drop his entire life to come clean out my home, or chauffer me around to meetings, or be *my* designated driver! You never tell me you're proud of me. You never insist I don't have to worry about anything when *I* fail at something." The anger evaporated and was replaced with sadness as she shook her head, dark curls swaying around her face. "I'll never be good enough for you." Her voice hitched and cracked as she swallowed back the breakdown. There'd be time to fall apart later. Squaring her shoulders and jutting her chin, she brought her tirade to a close. "You've played favourites my entire life and now...well, now I'm *done*."

In the tense silence which followed, every instinct in her bones screamed at her to turn on her heel and storm out, but she held firm. Her mother's jaw worked as she stared back at Rosie in horror. But, after a moment, Meredith's expression smoothed back out into haughty disdain.

"If that's how you feel, Rosemary," she sniffed dismissively, "you can show yourself out."

Oddly, the words didn't hurt. A strange emptiness filled Rosie instead. She nodded. "Fine."

Rosie left the room to the sounds of her father attempting to talk some sense into her mother, and with shaking hands she texted Liv once she had ordered an Uber to take her home.

'*Well that's been brewing for at least the decade I've known you,*' Liv replied, followed by, '*Are you okay?*'

Was she? Rosie wasn't sure. She was no longer upset, but she wondered if that might be shock. Or perhaps by airing all she had held inside for years, her anger and pain was replaced by relief. Not wanting to worry her friend, though, she told her she was okay and that she'd see her at the wedding the next day.

A text from Micah came through as she was unlocking her front door, after having successfully evaded her creepy neighbour whose name she still couldn't recall on her way into the building. '*If you want to run away to the US with me, you can.*'

It was potentially the sweetest thing he had ever said to her.

…And an incredibly tempting offer.

Chapter Thirteen

"His Best Man is Everett Rhodes," Micah repeated in an astonished tone for the fifth time, hissing the words under his breath. To his left sat Liv, and Rosie was to his right with Rob on her other side. The ceremony, which was underway, was being held in a stunning rooftop garden overlooking Surfers Paradise, an oceanfront suburb and tourist hub of Queensland's Gold Coast.

Rosie kicked her brother's ankle. "For the last time, shut up," she hissed back.

Micah had befriended Brennan during his first and only year of university. It had been Brennan who had encouraged Micah to pursue his dreams instead of working on a degree he had zero interest in. Rosie knew Micah had always looked up to his friend, and that he was probably hurt that his friend hadn't forewarned him that the Best Man was a famous actor.

Not that she could blame Brennan, either. While Micah's intentions were usually good, he would have been like a dog with a bone once he found out about a potential opportunity to network his way into Hollywood.

Micah made a huffing sound and folded his arms across his chest. "Just sayin' he could have told me he knew the guy."

Rolling her eyes, Rosie turned her attention back to the couple getting married. Both men looked handsome as ever. With his raven-coloured hair styled back from his face, Jeff wore a black suit and vest, and finished the ensemble with an emerald tie, a colour that matched the colours of

138

his wedding party. The Maid of Honour and the other groomsmaid wore identical emerald green rockabilly style dresses, and his groomsman wore a suit similar to Jeff's, but without a vest. Brennan wore a grey suit and vest with the same green tie and the three men at his side dressed the same way, but without vests. Both Brennan and Jeff were beaming at each other while the celebrant spoke about their lives together.

Rosie was incredibly happy for them. She was. But there was a tiny part of her which wondered if she might ever get to the same point in her life. Would she ever find that sort of happiness? Would she ever radiate pure joy for someone, the way Brennan and Jeff were for each other?

She was more than aware of Rob's comforting presence beside her, but she shoved down the instinct to lean into him. They'd agreed he would accompany her as a friend, and she had been the one to insist on that so she had no right to confuse him by changing the rules unexpectedly. But damn if he wasn't the person she imagined standing across from her in her very own Happily Ever After.

Which was weird, right? She'd only known him a few weeks…did people fall in love that quickly? Or was this all part of her clingy personality?

Shaking the thoughts from her head before she could go too far down the rabbit hole, she shifted her gaze to the object of Micah's ranting. Brennan's Best Man – actor Everett Rhodes. That really *was* a surprise. He stood beside Brennan just as attractive as he appeared on television, with his dark hair in his trademark coif and his cheeks covered in his famously trimmed stubble. He couldn't keep his blue eyes off Gemma, Brennan's sister (and Jeff's Maid of Honour), or the little girl currently propped on her hip. The little girl with long, dark hair and wide blue eyes which matched his.

Rosie's eyes widened.

Holy shit!

Gemma's kid was Rhodes's kid.

The realisation had her shifting back in her seat, stunned. She could definitely understand why Brennan hadn't said anything to Micah now. If she'd still been working at the blog, she would have been sacked for knowingly withholding her access to exclusive celebrity gossip if Margot had ever found out. Thank God she'd quit! Making a mental note to let Gemma know as much, Rosie waved off the concerned glance Rob was sending her, feeling doubly glad that she'd asked him to be her date instead of Grant.

The grooms exchanged their vows, the celebrant declared them officially married, and Rosie got to her feet and applauded as the newlyweds and the wedding party walked back down the aisle. Micah barely restrained himself from launching out of his seat to confront his friend. Liv held him back for extra measure, reminding him that it wasn't the time.

"Come on," Rosie sighed, nudging her brother's shoulder with her own, "let's go congratulate them, then do the obligatory group photos thing." She grinned teasingly. "You *like* the photos thing." Micah wasn't shy of the spotlight, after all.

"Besides," Rob offered, causing their entire little group's eyes to lock on to him, "you're more likely to network with Rhodes if you're not causing a scene, right?"

Rosie smirked at her date and mouthed 'thank you' as Micah visibly processed the argument.

"Yeah, that's a fair point," Micah acknowledged, nodding at Rob. "You're alright, Rando."

Rosie hung her head, her cheeks burning. Neither Micah nor Liv had made any secret of their curiosity where Rob was concerned.

To his credit, Rob merely smirked and shot Rosie a brief, conspiratorial wink, "I prefer Roberto."

At that, her cheeks burned for a different reason. Thankfully, though, the discussion moved on as they joined the queue of people clambering to congratulate the newlyweds.

"Gemma and Sara's dresses are gorgeous," Rosie told Liv as she glanced over at the women in question.

The wedding party had dispersed as they waited for the photographer to take individual photos of the new husbands with their various guests. Gemma and her best friend Sara, who Rosie only knew from having met her at a handful of Brennan's get-togethers, had been joined by Everett Rhodes and a taller, broader blond-haired man.

Liv chuckled. "Screw their dresses. Their *dates* are gorgeous."

"Hey," Micah complained, "I'm right here."

"Nobody said you weren't also pretty, Mike, calm down." Rosie patted his arm consolingly.

He rolled his eyes. "Calm down? This coming from the tantrum queen?"

Oh no. They were not discussing her recent explosions here. She scowled. "Don't."

"Did I miss something?" Rob interrupted, looking between Micah and Rosie.

She shook her head. "I'll explain later."

The group in front of them finished up hugging and congratulating Brennan and Jeff and, to ward off any further discussion of her outbursts, Rosie surged forward and hugged Brennan enthusiastically.

"Congratulations!" She beamed as they pulled apart and she moved aside to hug Jeff. "Your vows were beautiful. I think I hate you both."

They laughed and then Jeff looked over her shoulder, jutting his chin in Rob's direction. Rob had hung back, presumably to give Micah and Rosie a proper chance to talk to their friends. He was clean shaven and sharply dressed in a suit which Micah had whistled at earlier, likely because it was designer. Jeff's appraised Rob before he asked, "Who's this?"

On cue, Rob stepped forward, and Rosie introduced him to Brennan and Jeff as 'my friend Rob' in as much of a casual tone as she could possibly muster up. She was not oblivious to their raised eyebrows or their silent conversation before they each shook Rob's hand and thanked him for coming.

Micah broke the awkwardness, though, by nonchalantly asking, "So, how'd you manage to con Everett Rhodes into being your Best Man?"

Brennan had the grace to appear a little sheepish. "Sorry, man, I know I should have told you, but…" he trailed off with a shrug, casting a quick glance in Rosie's direction.

She held up her hands in surrender. "I quit the whole entertainment blogger thing," she informed him. "It was soul crushing."

"Good for you!" Jeff cheered. "And it'll be a relief for Gems and Rhett, I'm sure."

"I wouldn't have written about them anyway, I swear." She tried not to feel too insulted that they had assumed otherwise.

"You mightn't have had the choice," Brennan shrugged, before he shook off his serious tone and grinned. "But I'm glad to hear you're out of it, regardless. Where are you working now?"

"Well…" she began, but the photographer unapologetically interrupted.

"We're losing sunlight, so we need to hurry it along if you want to get all the group photos taken and still make it to the beach for wedding party shots."

Rosie stepped back. "We'll catch up later," she acknowledged, shooing them towards the photographer, "enjoy your wedding!"

As all the guests were herded together for the group photos, Rosie watched as Brennan was swamped by his family's hugs. She felt a mild pang of jealousy which she stamped down on as best she could. She was there to support her friends and celebrate with them, not focus on the life she'd wished she had.

Still, her smiles were forced for the camera, and she looked forward to imbibing a glass of wine or three at the reception.

* * *

Brennan and Jeff's reception was even more beautiful than the ceremony had been. The large function room they'd hired within the hotel was bedecked with fairy lights, pristine white linen and emerald green sashes over the backs of the chairs. Dinner was sublime, and the large dance floor called to the guests like a siren.

Despite the desire to drown her sorrows in wine, Rosie sipped at a single glass of champagne during the speeches - laughing her way through both Gemma's and Rhodes's, as Maid of Honour and Best Man respectively, alongside the rest of the guests - and stuck with lemonade for the rest of the evening. She didn't think getting blind drunk while she was still feeling emotionally off kilter on the tail of finally blowing up at her mother was a good idea.

What had been a good idea, though, was inviting Rob along. He seemed to find socialising with strangers easy, and he charmed the other guests at their table within moments. But, even while he was effortlessly schmoozing, he stayed by Rosie's side with an arm casually slung around her shoulders. Every so often he'd ask if she was having fun, or if she needed another drink, and without fail, every time he did, butterflies fluttered in Rosie's belly.

He was such a good man.

Case in point: that very moment he was looking at her with a soft smile. "Want to dance?"

She didn't deliberate. The offer was too good to pass up. Grinning and tossing her napkin over her plate, she took his proffered hand. "Please."

Rob led the way to the dance floor where they joined half of the other guests. He appeared to have no qualms bopping away to the strains of Beyoncé's '*Single Ladies*', making sassy arm movements and all.

"The brunette groomsmaid looks like she's going to strangle your brother," he informed her midway through the dance, causing Rosie to look over in the direction he was gesturing.

Sure enough, Sara was rolling her eyes and attempting to not-so-subtly guide Micah away from the table where the wedding party were seated. Rosie didn't need to listen in to know that her brother was attempting to 'network' with the unexpected Hollywood connection in their midst.

"Ugh," Rosie sighed, sashaying her hips to a round of '*oh oh oh*'s in the lyrics, "should I go help?"

"He's a big boy." Rob stepped in closer, shaking his head, "You're not his keeper, regardless of whatever your parents have told you."

"Just my mother," she corrected him, and then frowned. She hadn't told him too much about her family dynamic – that was the one thing she'd kept private, not wanting to scare him off completely. Stopping her movements, she arched an eyebrow at him. His words were ones she'd heard frequently. "Liv?"

Also stopping, Rob shrugged unapologetically. "Yeah. While you were in the loo she interrogated me, then gave me the 'hurt my best friend, I'll castrate you' spiel." His smile quickly cut into the frustration she felt and instead made her a weak-kneed, as it always did. Damn that dimple. "It was sweet," he concluded.

"Except I told her we're just friends. She has no idea what she's talking about." If anything, Rosie was the one toying with Rob's feelings. *She* was the one who couldn't make up her damn mind on what she wanted in life or love. Not *him*. "And if *anyone* has the right to unload my family drama on you, it should be me, not her."

"Easy." Rob coaxed her like she was some sort of wild beast that needed calming, holding his hands up in surrender. "She meant well. And, to be honest, I'm glad she told me."

Rosie blinked at him. "What?"

She barely registered that the music had changed to a slow song, but Rob pulled her into his arms and they swayed together amongst the other couples. Out of the corner of her eye, she watched as Gemma led her actor boyfriend across the room and onto the dance floor a few metres away, well and truly out of Micah's range.

"Well…" Rob's voice had her attention zeroing back in on him and her heart began to beat a little faster at the soft look on his face. "It explained a lot. And also made me feel pretty damn guilty for trying to push you into something you're not ready for."

Her cheeks flushed; Rosie gave her head another shake. "No! No – you weren't pushy. I just…" she swallowed roughly and looked away again, now watching as Rhodes and Gemma's little girl giggled madly as she was twirled around the dance floor by the blond man Rosie had been introduced to as Charlie Rhodes: Everett's brother and Sara's boyfriend. They seemed like a close-knit family unit, and it made Rosie more than a little jealous. She lowered her voice, feeling the tightness in her chest as she finished her sentence, "I told you I was messed up."

"Hey." Rob reached under her chin and gently directed her to look at him. His blue-grey eyes were warm and understanding. "We're all messed up in our own ways. I'm still in the wrong for-"

His words were cut off abruptly as Rosie pressed her lips to his.

Rosie closed her eyes as planted a soft, gentle kiss on Rob's lips. She couldn't help herself! There was something about him which undid all her resolve. She could taste the remnants of beer on his lips, could smell the spicy, earthy, soothingly familiar scent of his aftershave on his skin, and delighted in the way his hands tightened their hold on her back as he sank into the kiss.

Until he tensed and pulled back.

"Rosie," he murmured. Her heart thudded in her chest painfully because his tone set off warning bells in her head.

It wasn't the sort of tone one wanted to hear when they'd just taken an emotion-fuelled leap of faith and kissed the perfect man in front of oneself. No. It sounded regretful and cautious. The sound of a gentle letdown.

"This isn't a good idea," he finished. Rosie immediately felt a flush of embarrassment creep up her neck and over her cheeks.

Face burning, she could feel her throat tightening with impending tears. *Another stellar choice, Rosemary.*

But Rob was holding her close, his arms firm around her. He seemed determined to say his piece before Rosie could flee and hide and drink her weight in wine. "You said it yourself: you've got stuff to sort out before we can give it a proper go, and I don't want to fuck that up."

Well, damn it. How was she supposed to argue with that?

Rosie forced herself to meet his eyes; he smiled down at her ruefully. "Trust me," he continued, seemingly confident that she wouldn't turn tail and run anymore, because he moved one hand so he could reach up to tuck a lock of her hair behind her ear gently. "There's nothin' I want more than to pick up right where we left off, but that's not fair to either of us."

A tear slid down Rosie's cheek, cooling a track along the skin that had been heated by her blushing. He brushed the tear aside with his thumb. Rosie took a deep breath and attempted to apologise. "I'm-"

"Babe, if you say 'sorry'..." Rob trailed off, not finishing the threat. He pressed his forehead to hers and murmured, "It's an emotional day. It sounds like you've had a pretty rough few weeks...not to mention the last few days on their own, according to Liv. Who, by the way, is glaring at me pretty hard right now."

This information, delivered dryly, was enough to startle a watery laugh out of Rosie. She pulled back and turned to her right to see Liv arching an eyebrow at her from the table she and Micah had been seated at. Rosie shook her head and mouthed 'Later' at her best friend before meeting Rob's gaze again. "Still, I-"

"*You*," he cut her off again, giving her a reassuring squeeze, "are only human. You're at a wedding. Everyone's loved up. And I backed you into a proverbial corner by bringing up another emotional topic. I'd have kissed me, too," he said with a crooked smile.

It sucked that he could read her so well. It wasn't as though they had even known each other for that long. But he was a lawyer who specialised in contract law – his attention to detail was impeccable. There was no sense arguing with him when his observations were correct. However, it just made her feel all the more embarrassed for her moment of weakness.

"Hey." Rob's voice was soft and soothing, murmured against the shell of her ear as he guided her to rest her head on his shoulder. He led them in a facsimile of a dance, swaying gently to the music. "Don't go getting worked up about it. I'd rather you kissed me than anyone else." He sighed. "And it's killing me to not go with it, but I don't want you to regret it. I want us - when there is an us - to work out."

Rosie chuckled a little at his pronouncement, proud that the sound that came out of her throat was more amused than watery now. "*When*, huh?" she asked. "Pretty sure of yourself there, *Roberto*."

His lips ghosted over her temple; she could feel them pull into a smirk against her skin. "I thought confidence was an attractive quality?"

"You keep telling yourself that." It felt nice to be sinking back into flirting. To know that her impulsive, reckless decision to throw herself back at him hadn't ruined everything between them. She still wasn't quite sure what Rob saw in her, but she was glad he was so understanding and patient.

They continued to dance through the next song, and Micah and Liv appeared at their side midway through it. The music was fun and uplifting, and it was easy to forget her troubles as she watched the others competing with one another for silliest dance moves. When Rosie eventually begged off, yawning, Rob offered to walk her up to the room which she was sharing with her brother in the hotel.

She had to admit: Micah really had thought of everything when he'd gone

146

ahead and RSVPed for her.

In the comfortable silence between them, Rosie flashed back to the ill-attempted kiss and cringed. The carpeted hallway cushioned their footfalls, so her voice sounded louder than she'd intended when she spoke. "Thank you again for tonight. For...for being my date and being good about the whole humiliating myself thing."

They were still a few doors down from her room, but Rob stopped her and shook his head. "You didn't humiliate yourself. Well, at least not until you did the Chicken Dance." They both chuckled again, and he smiled softly as the moment passed. "I'm gonna be waiting for you for as long as you need. And I'll still be your friend, even if you decide...well, even if somethin' between us isn't actually gonna happen, okay?"

"Okay." She nodded. Relief settled over her as Rob's quietly spoken declaration warmed Rosie. He really was working hard to prove that he didn't want to pressure her. Perhaps learning about how poorly she handled being guilted into things really had been a wake-up call for him. She should probably thank Liv for that. Once she finished strangling her.

They made it the last few paces to her door just as Rob asked, "Have you given much thought to what you'll do next?"

It was such a loaded question. It was certainly not the sort of thing to bring up right when they were about to part ways. But she hadn't had a chance to talk to anyone about it, not since she'd blown up at her mother, and Rosie suddenly wanted to talk it out. She felt that if she didn't, she might combust.

Swiping the key card through the door's electronic reader, she pushed the heavy timber open and gestured for Rob to go in ahead of her, much to his obvious surprise. She shrugged. "How's about I make a couple of crappy instant coffees first?"

He followed her inside, where Rosie proceeded to unload everything on him. The words spilled forth from her lips: she explained her history with her mother, told him about her hopes and dreams, and about the tailspin her life seemed to be taking. Her shoulders felt lighter with every secret shared. Rob held her through tears, murmured encouragement, and asked questions to help organise her thoughts.

He didn't push his own opinions or feelings on her, though she knew he had to have them. The way he tensed as she explained the pressure she had been under from her mother, from Damian, from Margot – that seemed to be more than just an empathetic reaction. But he hadn't told her what she ought to do, only asked her to consider how she felt. She didn't think she'd ever be able to repay him for the kindness and support.

Micah stumbled in on them an hour later.

"What the hell?" he asked.

Rosie took stock of what it was he was seeing. She and Rob were cuddled up together on top of the cream coloured covers of her double bed with their backs against the headboard. However, she knew it would be obvious that she'd been crying, and she didn't need her brother leaping to the wrong conclusions.

"We were just talking, Mike," she informed him as she scrubbed her hand over her face and grimaced as she realised she'd smeared her mascara over her skin. She shot Rob a grateful smile. "I had a lot I needed to get off my chest."

Micah tossed his jacket and tie onto the back of the spare chair by the tiny breakfast table where Rob's jacket and tie had been draped carefully over the other. He flopped unceremoniously onto the other bed. It was separated from the one she had chosen by a single bedside table. The room itself was modern, but minimalist. They hadn't needed anything fancy for a single night's stay, after all.

Rolling onto his side, Micah observed Rosie seriously. "The offer still stands. You wanna come to the States with me? Run away for a little while?"

It was still a very tempting offer.

Chapter Fourteen

"I miss you."

Rob had barely answered the phone before Rosie had spoken. Since he'd accompanied her to her friends' wedding, their friendship had only grown stronger. Unfortunately, so had his feelings for her.

Even over a month later, he kicked himself for not just going with it when she had kissed him at the wedding. Oh, he knew he had made the right call at the time. Taking advantage of an emotionally vulnerable woman had never been his modus operandi. However, all he'd been able to imagine since they'd parted was the feel of her lips on his, the way her soft curves moulded against his body, and the gentle floral scent of her perfume. He'd wanted her naked six ways to Sunday even then, and the time apart hadn't helped him get over that at all.

He recalled lying next to her in the quiet of her hotel room, listening while she talked through the pros and cons of her options. It had been so tempting to tell her what *he* wished she'd do - choices which would benefit him - but he hadn't. He'd forced himself to encourage her to do whatever it was that would make her happy, even if it meant she might take up her brother's offer and move half-way around the world, well and truly out of his own reach.

She'd been grateful for his support, even while he had kicked himself for not fighting harder for what he wanted.

It felt strange not doing so.

As a lawyer, he was naturally inclined to defend his own interests above all others.

Why hadn't he done so with Rosie?

You know why, a little voice in his head trilled in a sing-song sort of way. *You care about her.*

At least his brain hadn't leapt towards the 'L' word. He was a lawyer. He had to be rational and reasonable.

After all, 'love' wasn't rational, was it? Not when he and Rosie had only known each other a few weeks at the time of the wedding. It didn't matter how many times they'd slept together, though he had fond memories of the week he'd spent chasing her around Stefan's farmhouse, fucking her at every possible opportunity. No. Love took more than that, didn't it?

Of course, the traitorous leaping of his heart into his throat at her declaration when he'd answered the phone said otherwise.

"I miss you too, sweetheart." Rob was walking a tightrope at that point. They had become close friends, but he didn't want her to forget that he would happily be more when she was ready. Without pushing her, of course, because she didn't need the additional pressure. He smiled softly and got up to close his office door, the universal signal that he didn't want to be disturbed. "Are you still happy there?"

"I am." He could hear the smile in Rosie's voice. Admittedly, she sounded genuinely relaxed. "And I've written almost half of my first draft already."

At both his and her friends' encouragement, Rosie had begun writing a novel in her down time. Partially for cathartic reasons, but also because her dream had always been to become a novelist. With her mother no longer talking her out of it, Rosie had taken the dive back into creative writing like a duck to water.

"Whoa, already?" He felt a swell of pride in his chest. "You're made for this, babe."

"Meh." An awkward chuckle met his ears; Rob could picture her cheeks flushing. Rosie struggled with accepting praise and compliments, so Rob made an effort to shower her with them at every opportunity. "It's probably half rubbish that'll be cut during editing, but-"

"No. Stop it." Rob interrupted, wishing he was at her side and able to throw an arm around her shoulders and give her a comforting squeeze. He wanted to reassure her. Hold her. Support her in person. He frowned out the window at the oncoming twilight, watching streetlights turn on as darkness approached. "How many other people can churn out thirty to forty thousand words within a few weeks? You're talented, Rose. Own it."

"You haven't read it!" She argued, but he could hear her smile again.

"Then send it to me."

She sucked in an audible breath at his challenge. "I...I couldn't."

"Why not? Complete strangers read your writing online for years." It turned out that he and his sister had been among them. Belinda would call it 'fate' when he finally told her about Rosie, he just knew it.

He didn't think he could be blamed for keeping his 'friendship' with the former blogger to himself, but it had been developing for over a month at that point, and he knew his time was running out. And, really, some part of him (the same part that used the 'L' word) *wanted* to talk to his big sister about his feelings. He just wanted to be on more solid footing with Rosie before he said anything.

Speaking of Rosie, he forced himself to focus on the conversation again.

"Yeah," Rosie said in response to his argument, "when I was writing clickbait." She turned quiet and contemplative. "I actually care about this, and...and I care about your opinion...and if you read it and it's crap-"

"It's not going to be." He could feel it in his gut. She was too clever and witty for her words to be anything other than entertaining. "But I'll wait until you've edited, if that'll make you feel better."

Rosie was silent for a moment. "But you'll still give me honest feedback, right?"

"Always, sweetheart."

"Okay."

The conversation moved on and when they hung up, Rob sighed and shook his head, and then startled at the amused, "Sweetheart, huh?" spoken from the other side of his office.

He spun his chair so quickly he thought he'd given himself whiplash.

"Belinda!" He scowled at his sister; he was instantly reminded of when he'd been a teenager and Lindy had listened in on his phone calls to high school girlfriends. Any charitable thoughts he might have had about his sister were immediately forgotten. "What the fuck?"

Completely unrepentant, Lindy crossed the office and dropped into one of the two chairs in front of his desk. "I was going to ask you to join me for dinner, but now I'm telling you to." She leaned forward, grinning widely. "Who is 'sweetheart', and why is this the first I'm hearing of her?"

"Lindy, it's not quite what you think." He cursed himself for not being able to keep the longing from his voice while he spoke to Rosie: clearly his equally attentive to detail big sister leapt on it.

With her index finger pointed at him in both victory and accusation, she assessed, "But you want it to be."

Shoulders slumping in defeat, Rob sighed and scrubbed his hand over his face. "Yeah, well, it's not up to me."

An expression which he hadn't seen since he was a kid passed over her features, and the fierce mama bear glimmer in her eyes lingered as she drummed her fingers on the desk's surface. "She's not stringing you along, I hope."

"I'm a big boy," he reminded her gently, "and I can look out for myself. But, for your information, no. It's not like that, either. It's-"

"If you're about to say 'complicated' like a cry for help Facebook relationship status…"

While she let the threat hang, unfinished, he laughed. "How about 'there's a bit to work out first', then?"

Settling back in her chair, his sister folded her arms across her chest and lifted an eyebrow. "Oh, you are *so* telling me the whole story, buster."

And even though he was annoyed with her for eavesdropping, he did.

It felt good to talk to his big sister about it. Explaining his and Rosie's instant connection was easy. Their banter, their campfire discussions, and the unexpected - but wholly welcomed - sex. "It was only supposed to be the one night…but then we met again at Stefan's farm."

His sister sat up straighter, having followed his story so far with empathy and amusement. "Stefan? As in my soon-to-be brother-in-law Stefan?"

"How many other Stefans do you reckon I know?" He paused for a moment, allowing the question to sink in. "And then how many d'you think have farms?"

Belinda frowned at him. "Point." She cocked her head. "I'll ask him later why he didn't spill the tea on your new love interest." Rolling her wrist at him, she added, "You can keep going."

Darkness had settled outside by this stage, but the office was still brightly lit. Rob squinted as he turned his head to stare out of his window, down over the street. Cars drove past in a steady stream, their headlights causing the Norfolk pines to cast long, spikey shadows over the road and footpath. It was still a nice view, even at night, but his heart was elsewhere.

"So, we reconnected," he continued, a soft smile lifting his lips at the recollection of a week spent making love at every opportunity. The feel of her curves in his hands, her supple breasts, her wickedly talented tongue. If he hadn't already fallen for her, the week at the farm had pushed him over the edge. "But I knew from the start that she was in a bit of a rough place in her life." He glanced back at his sister. "Family issues. Career stalled, that sort of thing." Lindy nodded sympathetically. "So forcing her into more than she was ready for wasn't fair."

"Always a gentleman, huh?"

Once again he flashed back to the wedding. To Rosie's lips on his. To the expression of hurt and embarrassment on her face when he'd gently turned her down. Still, he'd meant every word he had said. As desperately as he'd wanted to drag her up to her room and show her how desirable she was, he wanted more than just a fling with Rosemary Weiss, and she had not been ready. "Unfortunately."

"There's a story there, I'm guessing?"

"Not one I'm gonna tell."

Knowing just how far she could push him, his sister backed off that particular line of questioning, her hands held in surrender. "Okay, okay. I'll leave it for now." Her knowing smile was back, though, as she prodded, "But you're still talking, obviously."

With a roll of his eyes, he gave in and shut his laptop down. He then pushed the lid closed and slipped the entire device into his laptop satchel, rose to his feet, and shoved his phone into his hip pocket. "Come on," he ordered, rounding the desk and crossing the room. His hand hovered over the light switch as he waited for Belinda to follow him out. "I'm starving. You can continue interrogating me over dinner."

"Shit, hey?" Lindy chuckled, waiting patiently for him to set the alarms and lock the main door. "You really are serious about this one."

The non-committal sound from the back of his throat didn't convince either of them.

His sister's grin widened and she squeezed his bicep. "Okay, so you're giving me *all* the details, and then I wanna meet her."

"You're jumping ahead again," he accused without any heat. "But, yeah, you'd like her, I think."

Or, at least, he'd hoped.

But there he was, leaping ahead. When had he become such a sentimental bastard, anyway?

* * *

"Your book is fantastic, sweetheart," the endearment left Rob's lips before he could stop it, but he was too worked up to care. Three weeks after he had assured her that he wanted to read it when it was done, Rosie had sent him the completed first draft of her novel. When he had finally sat down to read it, he'd devoured the entire book within a couple of hours. It was a good thing it was a Saturday! "I couldn't put it down."

On the other end of their Facetime call, Rosie's cheeks were turning pink. "It's just a first draft," she argued, and once again Rob wanted to strangle whoever had broken her to the point of being unable to take a simple compliment. Tucking a curly lock of hair behind her ear, she shrugged. "It needs a serious edit, and a good chunk of it needs to be rewritten."

"Stop it," he demanded. "Stop downplaying how well you've done."

"I'm not-"

"You are! You've written eighty thousand words within six weeks, and they're *good*, babe. Really good."

It honestly had astounded him that he'd enjoyed the novel as much as he had. Romance was not his genre, but Rosie had tempered it with humour and suspense. Rob wasn't sure how Rosie was going to market it – it was like a crime novel, complete with gunfights and kidnappings, but also hilarious and slapstick. And the sex scenes? Well, Rob was distinctly aware that the brooding hero of the book sounded very similar to the man who looked back at him in the mirror every day. So if he'd been aroused while reading, it wasn't his fault. Rosie had practically told him exactly what she needed from him but had couched it in fiction.

Clever girl.

"And the smut wasn't stupid?" she asked, biting at her thumbnail anxiously, unaware of the path his thoughts had taken, but somehow in tune with them. "I've never written sex scenes before."

Without thinking, he informed her, "I got so hard after the scene in the fifth chapter, I needed to-"

Her gasp cut off his admission, her hands covering her mouth while the pink on her cheeks turned into a deep red. "Rob!"

"As if you didn't write that for me." He channelled his courtroom persona: cocky and knowing. "Detective Mack Anderson sounded very familiar, Rose. Dark hair cut in a more-on-top style…" here he ran a hand through his own, illustrating his point, "…steely grey-blue eyes, stubble, and a penchant for the outdoors? Sweetheart, you had to know I'd make the connection real quick."

"Fuck," she muttered under her breath, her face betraying her embarrassment again. After heaving a sigh, she shrugged. "Yeah. Alright. You've got me. It's not like you don't know that I find you attractive."

On the contrary, Rob knew that Rosie's feelings ran deeper than simply physical attraction, considering their history to date. But he wasn't pushing her. He refused to do that to her. Enough people in her life already had.

"*Mmm*, and the scene out in the log cabin was *brilliant*, babe. The whole witness protection, no outside contact, them against the world vibes were great." He'd had flashbacks to the cottages at Stefan's farm, and he knew,

155

without Rosie having to say anything, that the locale was exactly what had inspired the scenes in her novel. "Pity we never got to make use of the rug in front of the fireplace in the cottage at Stefan's, eh?"

Even as he spoke the words, he could picture it. Frost covering the double-glazed windowpanes as well as the grass outside, while the space inside the little timber room was toasty and warm. Warm enough for him to lay her down on the soft rug in front of the hearth, the flickering of the flames highlighting her smooth, olive-toned curves. He imagined that the only sounds would be the crackling of the fire itself and their mutual heavy breathing. The slide of sweat-slicked bodies moving against each other. Her gasps and mewls as he took her to new heights.

God, he wanted to put the fantasy into action and bring it to life.

"Rob…" Her warning tone brought his thoughts careening back into reality. A reality where there was a physical distance between them, and she hadn't yet told him she wanted to take him up on his promise.

But still he was waiting.

He'd expected Pete to call him out on it when he'd finally told his best friend about Rosie. To point out how soft and pathetic he was being. But Pete had surprised him, clapping him on the shoulder and acknowledging that the special ones were worth waiting for.

Pete had also muttered something derisive about Rob finally growing up, but Rob had chosen to ignore that part.

Rosie *was* worth waiting for.

He'd known it from the moment he'd caught her swearing at her uncooperative tent. She'd been cute. Sassy. A little awkward. Not at all apologetic about who she was. At least, not with him. And *she* had made the first move.

Rob knew he was attractive. He wasn't above using his genetically gifted aesthetic to manipulate situations into going his way. Most of the women he'd been with over the years had fawned over his strong jaw and steely-blue eyes, all deferring to him and his interest in them, waiting it out until he made the first move.

But not Rosie.

No. She had known what she'd wanted, and she'd gone for it, and *damn* if he didn't think it was the hottest thing to ever fucking happen to him. With her curves and her chocolate-coloured eyes and the mop of thick, silky soft curls atop her head…she was everything he hadn't known he desperately wanted.

And she had proven to be witty and flirtatious. She'd easily kept up with his banter in the days where he hadn't known that she was Stefan's new hire, and once they'd discovered the connection? Rereading their emails had been even more entertaining.

She was the whole package. Rob wasn't stupid enough to let her become 'the one who got away' just because the timing wasn't yet right.

If he'd learned anything from *The Tortoise and The Hare* when he'd been a kid, it was that being slow and steady could win the race…and this was one he was determined to win.

Bringing himself back to the warning in her tone, he shrugged apologetically at the iPad he'd propped up on his dining table in his apartment. "I'm sorry," he offered with genuine contrition. The smile he shot her was rueful. "I just got excited. But you say the word and I'm yours, Rosie."

He watched her expression as closely as he could on the small screen. For a moment, he read obvious yearning, but it melted away, replaced by something akin to doubt and disappointment. "You can do better than me," she murmured, before shaking her head and adding, "and I'm so far away…"

"That first part's bullshit." Rob's heart began beating harder in his chest. "But…are you saying that if I was there, you'd be ready to give us a go?"

Rosie nibbled on her lip.

His hopes soared.

"I'm still working through stuff…" she prevaricated.

It still wasn't a 'no'.

"You'll always have shit to work through," he argued, leaning forward as his enthusiasm and confidence built. "We both will. 'Cos we're human and that's all part of life." He cocked his head to the side, trying to read her properly through the screen. "You've been so much happier these last couple of months. Look at what you've achieved! And I know you've still gotta deal with your mum and decide what comes next for your career, but, babe, I wanna be there for it. For all of it." Rob wanted to reach out, to hold her hand and squeeze. He had to settle with placing his hand on the side of the screen, though she couldn't see it. "As more than just your friend."

If reading Rosie's book had told him anything, it was that she wanted all the same things, too. Why else would the character she'd so blatantly based on him be a strong, alpha male protector type? She was too independent to ask for it, but she wanted him to be there as a support system in a way he didn't think she'd actually experienced in her life. And he wanted to be that person for her, if she would let him.

There was a moment of silence between them, and Rob worried that he might have pushed too hard, too soon. Then she visibly swallowed and asked, "When'll you be free to come out here, then?"

His car keys were in his hand before he knew it.

Chapter Fifteen

After Brennan and Jeff's wedding, Stefan had been waiting on the wraparound veranda when Rosie pulled her car up to its usual position at the farm. It had taken her a couple of weeks to pack away her old life, the remnants of which had travelled with her in boxes taking up her backseat, boot, and the back of Rob's Land Cruiser. Breaking her lease and making plans to move to the farm permanently had felt liberating.

Her boss-come-landlord/new housemate had jogged down the front steps as she climbed out of the car. "Welcome back!" Stefan had declared with exuberance. Rosie had squealed as Stefan pulled her into his arms and spun her around in a circle. Then he had stood back and grinned. "I've missed you."

When she'd called him to ask for her job back, Stefan had been more than happy to agree. She wasn't getting her old cabin, though. Because she wanted to work there permanently, Stefan had offered her a room in the main house. It wouldn't be as private, but the cabins weren't intended as a permanent use for staff - they were for bringing in extra income to the farm proper. As much as she would miss the cosiness, Rosie had understood. Besides, the main house was gorgeous and huge, and she was certain that she and Stefan wouldn't get under each other's feet.

It was nice to be needed.

Upon Rosie's arrival, Stefan had led her to the bedroom closest to the main bathroom and furthest from his master suite. It was a large bedroom with double doors that led onto the side veranda, and an inviting king-sized bed, dressed with the same pillow soft coverings as the bed in the cabin had been. On the side wall, next to the room's main door, stood an antique oak wardrobe, and a matching storage chest sat at the foot of the bed. The room was light and airy, with a bright, multi-coloured rug covering much of the polished timber floors.

From the moment she'd stepped foot into the space, it had already felt like home.

Rosie had gotten rid of her own furniture but felt as though she'd received an upgrade when she'd entered the room. And, in the weeks that followed, she hadn't once regretted her decision to move to the farm.

Well… she mused as she Facetimed with Rob, *except for when it comes to him.*

After her embarrassing display at Brennan's wedding and their ensuing deep and meaningful conversation, she would have understood if the insanely attractive man had wanted to cut and run. However, Rob had assured her he was sticking around as a friend, and that she hadn't scared him off.

Unfortunately, his sweet words had only caused more conflict within her.

At that point, Rosie had been fairly certain she was falling for him, and there he had gone, sealing the deal.

So, when Micah had suggested that she run away to America with him, she'd known her answer was going to be an emphatic refusal. As tempting as the offer had been, she was too attached to Rob and had genuinely wanted to see if she could sort her shit out enough to contemplate a real relationship with him. That had meant not leaving the country.

Instead, when Rob had asked her to close her eyes and think about what made her happiest, the image had come to her immediately.

Stefan's farm.

It was still too far away from Rob for her liking, but it was within the same country - the same state, even - which was a much more comfortable thought than going overseas. Besides, running away from her life wasn't going to solve anything, was it?

Working at the farm for long mightn't be her ultimate goal, but she knew she was her best self when she was there – something she had proven to herself in the time since she had returned. She'd even written an entire novel! In a matter of weeks, she had completed a life goal that had simmered under her skin since her early teens.

Was it cut-glass prose literature? No. But the words had flown from her fingertips, the story practically spinning itself as she tapped at the keys on her laptop every night in bed. Since returning to the farm, Rosie had felt energised in a way she couldn't ever recall feeling before. Refreshed. Determined.

Happy.

And I can attribute a lot of that to this guy, she mused, grinning at her phone screen as Rob's chair clattered to the floor on his end of the call.

He was wearing his usual weekend attire: jeans that showed off the perfect, squeezable shape of his butt, and a flannelette shirt worn open over a white t-shirt. The beginnings of his beard were growing back in again, the dark stubble highlighting the line of his strong, square jaw. He was just as handsome as ever. Perhaps even more so, with his eyes lit up like she'd just told him it was Christmas; a genuine smile stretched across his face.

"Are you serious?" he was practically bouncing on the balls of his feet.

Now that she had asked him to come, it felt as though a weight had lifted from Rosie's shoulders. Rob had been so patient and understanding, never actually rushing her despite his flirtatious nature. A part of Rosie had wanted so badly to give in earlier, but she had needed the time she'd taken to reset herself and figure out what she genuinely wanted from life.

Writing the novel had been her subconscious's way of telling her that, no matter what, Rob was on that list. It should not have surprised her when he'd worked it out as well, considering his attention to detail and his knack for being able to read her so well.

As she nodded, Rosie could feel her face betraying the level of affection she felt for him. "I've never been more serious in my life."

On his end of the call, Rob gave a shout and dove out of the frame for a couple of seconds. Rosie could hear him rattling about in his apartment - a space which looked exactly as she'd imagined a wealthy bachelor pad on the Gold Coast would, with pristine white walls, white leather furniture, pale timber surfaces and chrome appliances - before the jangle of keys met her ears.

Rob reappeared on the screen, holding his keys up in victory. "I'll see you in a few hours, then." A lascivious wink followed. "*Do* wait up."

"What? You're driving out now?" She glanced at her bedside table, eyeing the clock and calculating that he would probably arrive after ten o'clock at night. "Rob…"

"You've got a snowball's chance in hell of talkin' me out of this, babe." His eyes were glinting with the promise of so many things, and his roguish grin completed the look. "Not when I know I get to kiss you once I'm there."

"Just kiss, huh?" They'd been talking about the smut she had written, smut that they both knew featured her desire for him. Rob's excitement to see Rosie made her feel giddy…and bold. "Seems like a long way to travel for *just* a kiss."

"Well," he leaned down to his camera, expression turning sinful as he lowered his voice, the deep, husky whisper lit goosebumps on Rosie's flesh, "I'm too much of a gentleman to tell you I also plan on fucking you so hard you forget your own name." He grinned wickedly. "Come to think of it, Stef should probably invest in some noise cancelling earphones or something."

Practically vibrating with anticipation, Rosie couldn't bring herself to be concerned with what Stefan might think, though she felt she should probably give him the head's up that Rob was on his way.

"Just drive carefully, then," she responded. "I'll be waiting for you, but I want you here in one piece."

He tipped an imaginary hat at the camera. "Yes, ma'am."

* * *

With her bedroom near the front of the house, Rosie heard the crunching of tyres on gravel heralding her visitor's arrival and enabling her to beat her housemate to the front door. Stefan and Rob could catch up in the morning.

For the evening, Rob was all hers.

The muted sound of the Land Cruiser's door closing had her wrenching the front door open to see her intended paramour rounding the side of the car with an overnight bag slung over his shoulder. The light from the house spilled out over the front steps and into his path, causing Rob to look up and break into a wide smile which made Rosie weak in the knees.

Even though she'd video-chatted with him hours earlier, she was not prepared for how attractive he was in the flesh, as was always the case.

"Hey stranger." Rosie leaned against the doorframe, her heart hammering in her chest. She couldn't quite believe this was real: that she had thrown caution to the wind and encouraged Rob to drive over three and a half hours to see her, *and* that he had done so without question. But there he was, his dark hair tousled from the wind, his stubble calling her to cup his strong jaw between her hands and kiss him like she'd never kissed anyone before.

"Hey yourself," he replied before jogging lightly up the front stairs and dropping his bag at her feet. "Miss me?"

Rosie rolled her eyes at the cheeky question and grabbed the open lapels of his flannelette overshirt, yanking him towards her without further preamble. She still wasn't sure what it was about Rob that brought out this previously undiscovered side of her, but she didn't care. She had a shitty hyper-emotional misplaced kiss to make up for, and she'd wasted enough time making attempts to get into the right state of mind for a shot at a real relationship when he seemed to care for her as she was, faults and all.

She tasted coffee when their tongues met – a dark, rich flavour that brought the rest of her senses zinging to life. With the warmth of his large hand at her back, and the other at her hip, she lost herself in rediscovering him. There was a subtle strength in the way he held her, comforting in ways she couldn't quite put words to. And, as always, his cologne had her olfactory senses on overdrive.

Rosie had no idea how long they stood there on the front veranda, wrapped around each other, but when Rob reluctantly pulled back and, in a voice roughened with need, informed her that they should head to her room, she led the way.

Letting him in ahead of her, she shut the door softly, then found herself gasping in surprise when she was pushed against the cool timber surface, bracketed in by Rob's strong arms on either side of her.

His lips hovered over hers, blue-grey eyes glinting with humour. "Wanna re-enact page one hundred and twelve?"

It made her giddy all over again to hear him referencing her writing. Some part of her wondered if that was narcissistic, but she'd already admitted that he had inspired the hero and a lot of the steamy scenes. She thought it was cute that he was so into it. Her lips brushed against his as she asked, "Which scene's that?"

"The scene where Mack rescued Dee from an attempted abduction and they're holed up in that shitty motel in the middle of nowhere."

In that moment, it struck her that his praise hadn't just been lip service. Rob genuinely had read the book from start to finish. He hadn't just skimmed it; he hadn't flipped through pages and picked sections to recite to her. He'd actually read it and followed the plot. Feeling a jumble of emotions, tears welled in her eyes. She blinked rapidly to clear them.

"Hey." Immediately, he sounded concerned. Pulling back, he cupped her face and gently ran his thumbs under her eyes, brushing away the moisture she hadn't quite been able to dispel. "What's wrong?"

She couldn't help but laugh at the question, shaking her head and bringing her hands up to cover his, where they were still gently cradling her face. "You're perfect," she answered. "You're perfect and I love you."

Before Rob sneaked into her campsite and her life, Rosie would have thought it ridiculous to feel so strongly for someone she'd never actually dated. But outside of their brief physical affair early on, they had spent months emailing, texting and exchanging calls as friends. Her feelings were deep, genuine, and strong. She loved him.

He blinked back at her, clearly surprised by the random, impromptu declaration.

Rosie suddenly realised that perhaps she was coming off a lot clingier and crazier than she actually felt. She averted her gaze, wondering how to fix her gaffe. "You don't have t-"

"Shut up," Rob's words were playful as his surprise dissipated. He then met Rosie's gaze steadily, his affection more than obvious. "I love you, too."

Rosie pulled him back in for another deep kiss. In response, Rob slotted a firm thigh between her legs and pressed her back into the doorway, making his intentions clear.

She chuckled into his mouth. "So…page one-twelve?"

"Oh, no, babe." he rested his forehead against hers. "We're going straight to the finale."

Before Rosie could even begin to consider what he meant, Rob's mouth was on hers again, initiating a deep, passionate kiss while he slowly turned them around and backed her towards the bed. There, he guided her down onto the mattress, crawled over her and slid his hands beneath her cotton pyjama top while he pressed kisses to her neck and jaw.

When his lips reached her ear, he practically purred, "Now, I know you've got a vibrator stashed around here somewhere."

A flush of arousal, tinged with mild embarrassment, crept up Rosie's chest and face. Despite her belief that there was absolutely nothing shameful about owning sex toys, it was one of those things she had always kept private. She wasn't even certain she had admitted to past lovers that she'd owned them.

But Rob's denim-clad erection was hard and insistent as it rested against her upper thigh, and she'd just been the most vulnerable with him that she had ever been with anyone. Hell, he had read the first draft of her novel. Admitting to her toy collection was *nothing* in comparison to any of those things.

"Bottom drawer," she whispered, gesturing vaguely to the bedside table closest to them. "There are a few."

It was nice to have variety.

She felt Rob's grin against her skin, the stubble scratching in all the best ways, before he rolled off her to rummage through the drawer in question.

"I like the look of this guy." Rob sat back on his knees and showed her his choice. It was her favourite of the three in her possession. Not the largest, but the one marketed as 'realistic', with a soft-touch silicone feel, and ten vibration settings. It was also rechargeable and waterproof. Old Faithful, if ever she'd known one. Rob played with the buttons, experimenting with the various settings as he smoothed his hand over its length in a motion Rosie found far too arousing to watch. "What's his name?"

"Mack," she answered without thinking, blushing as she realised just how much she'd given away.

There was a knowing glint in Rob's eyes, but he said nothing about the link between the character in her novel, and the toy, or whether there was any relation to him. However, he clearly couldn't resist saying, "That fills in some extra details for me." Whether he meant the novel, or who he imagined she fantasised about while fucking herself with the toy was anyone's guess. "Can Mack join us tonight?"

Rosie's brain just about short circuited.

None of her previous boyfriends had ever made this sort of suggestion before, perhaps because she had never even told those men that the toys existed. Either way, Rosie never really considered she'd been missing out on anything, but now, watching Rob handling her vibrator expertly, she felt as though her sex life to that point had been woefully lacking.

Moisture pooled between her thighs, her heart rate already increasing at the simple suggestion Rob had made. She ached: a deep, pulsing, needy ache for the man she had just confessed her love to. She wanted him inside her before she spontaneously combusted.

Nodding and swallowing roughly, she answered, "Please."

"Excellent." Rob set the toy down beside them on the bed, along with the small bottle of lube he'd also pilfered from her drawer. With how wet she already felt, Rosie didn't think it would be necessary, but she approved of his forethought, nonetheless. Following that, Rob dug into his hip pocket and pulled a condom from his wallet, the foil square joining the collection on the mattress while the wallet itself was tossed carelessly to the floor. Then he crawled back over Rosie with purpose, kissing her hungrily the second her lips were within his reach.

Arching up into Rob, Rosie pushed his open flannelette shirt over his shoulders and down his arms, assisting in his awkward efforts to remove it without breaking their kiss. Next, her hands slipped under his thin cotton t-shirt he. She skimmed over the toned, tanned abdomen and chest which she knew were concealed beneath, then moved around to his shoulders and down the firm, smooth plains of his back until her fingertips reached the band of his jeans.

Rob had slotted himself between Rosie's legs, which she had spread to accommodate him. Though they were both fully clothed, he rocked against her, causing her to become even more wet at the feel of his straining, jean-covered bulge.

"If you're not going to get naked soon, I'm going to have to take matters into my own hands," she threatened against his lips; to which he laughed.

"Patience, babe."

With a profound degree of incredulity, she asked, "Are you kidding me right now?"

He had driven three and a half hours the very moment she had told him she was ready to give a relationship a go. Even with the layers separating them, she could feel his cock practically throbbing as he pressed it against her pussy.

Rob moved back to kissing her neck, just below her jaw. She could hear his continued amusement as he declared, "We're savouring this, Rose."

Unable to contain her giggles as his whiskers tickled her skin, she swatted his ass. "It's not a one-time offer, you know. Treat it like a buffet. Go nuts."

One of his hands squeezed her hip affectionately. "You say the sweetest things," he joked. "Really setting the mood."

More laughter bubbled up and out of her. She felt light, happy, and carefree in ways she couldn't really recall feeling. Especially not during sex. But there she was, giggling and squirming beneath him, more comfortable than Rosie of the past would have thought she had any business feeling.

"Maybe you're not doing your job properly, then," she goaded.

Rob's chuckle was deep and rich and sent another rush of pure arousal straight through Rosie as he began to move back down her body, his hands and lips mapping a path over the skin he could reach. "You can't trick me into rushing."

Whatever playful response she was about to offer died on her tongue when Rob pushed up her pyjama top and began to mouth at the skin he was revealing. Licking and sucking a slow path to her breasts, Rob was clearly a man with a specific mission in mind.

Rosie inhaled sharply as Rob catalogued her ticklish spots then rubbed the scruff of his growing beard over them. He guided her to sit up for a moment and worked to remove her shirt completely, tugging it up and over her head before he discarded it across the room. Then he eased Rosie back down onto the mattress and hungrily eyed her bare breasts.

"Fuck, you're gorgeous," he enthused as he moved down her body again.

She'd spent the majority of her twenties learning to love her voluptuous body, despite society's general expectations that she conform to a different aesthetic. While none of her boyfriends had ever deliberately made her feel as though she wasn't enough (though she could now admit that some had made her question her self-worth regardless), there was something raw and genuine in the way Rob vocalised his attraction which squeezed her heart in all the best ways.

"Well…you know I think you are, too," she replied before nibbling her lip and watching his mouth descend on her left breast, his tongue teasing her nipple while darkened steely-blue eyes stared back up at her. The skin around them crinkled as the look in them turned wicked. Then she felt his teeth gently grazing her.

"*Oh,*" she breathed, fearing for the state of her underwear as she became impossibly drenched with her arousal. Almost unknowingly, she threaded fingers into his soft, thick hair, carefully holding his head in place. "Fuck. *Rob.*"

She lost herself in his ministrations, and then mewled in disappointment when he pulled away and cold air hit the moistened bud. But he repeated the attentions on her right breast which sent more jolts of pleasure through her.

Writhing beneath him, she reached between their bodies, the fingers of her right hand seeking out the button above the fly of his jeans, popping it before Rob realised what she'd done.

"Naughty," he accused, releasing her nipple and shifting his position again, moving his hips just out of her reach. "I'm really gonna take my time enjoying this now."

Despite his words, he shuffled further down the bed, pulling her pyjama pants and underwear down her legs as he went. She lifted her hips to ease the process, and was soon splayed out, naked and wanting, while he remained completely clothed.

"At least take your shirt off," she begged, reaching out in an attempt to help him do just that, but he sat back, grinning impishly.

"Patience," he repeated.

"Ugh." Rosie flopped backwards, her head meeting one of her pillows with a dull sound as she squeezed her eyes shut. "You're a fucking tease, *Roberto*."

She felt his hands smoothing up her calves, then over her knees and slowly up her thighs, spreading them further. God, if she'd thought she was dripping before, it was nothing in comparison to how she felt now, the anticipation making her body tense and quiver with anticipation.

Rob's thumbs rubbed slow, soothing circles over the inside of her parted legs. "You right?" he asked softly. Rosie swallowed roughly at the sensation of his breath ghosting over her exposed skin.

"You're killing me," she responded perhaps a beat too late as thoughts of the proximity of his mouth to where she needed attention most distracted her from his question. She opened her eyes and stared up at the ceiling, trying to will her heart rate down. He hadn't even touched her yet, and she was strung tighter than a bow. "Rob...*please*...I need...*That!* Right there. *Oh*, God, don't you dare stop."

She didn't know whether he'd just taken pity on her, or whether he'd been waiting for her to beg, but she didn't care. Licking a positively divine line from her dripping centre to her clit, Rob was finally giving her what she wanted. She sank back into the mattress with a relieved sigh, closing her eyes again in order to enjoy the exquisite bliss she knew his mouth and fingers would provide.

He lapped at her clit as he sank two fingers inside her, moaning appreciatively. Rosie rocked her hips, encouraging him to fuck her with them, and he didn't disappoint, adding a third not long after the first two, stretching her pleasantly as he scissored and curled them.

Rosie panted. Already the tell-tale tingles were starting. Her orgasm was within reach. She could almost taste it.

Then Rob removed his fingers.

"Wha…?" She began as she opened her eyes but cut herself off at the familiar buzzing sound. Her eyes widened. She'd forgotten about Mack.

But, instead of plunging the vibrator inside her, Rob pressed the tip to her clit and slid his tongue inside her instead.

It was a sensory overload.

Rosie writhed, a sheen of sweat building on her skin as the pleasure began to overwhelm her. Gripping the quilt beneath her, she was torn between focusing on the vibrations against her clit and the unparalleled feeling of his tongue fucking her while his free hand couldn't settle, sweeping over her hips, thighs, stomach, and snaking underneath her to squeeze and massage as it moved along.

Without warning, Rob switched things up again. He brought his mouth back to her clit, sucking at it and licking with additional pressure, and then slipped Mack inside her, turning the vibration setting to a constant high thrum. On the third slow thrust of the toy, Rosie cried out as she felt the mounting tension give way, a burst of light and pure pleasure crashing over her in a relentless wave.

She was dimly aware of Rob swapping Mack out again with his own mouth, practically drowning himself in her juices while her inner walls fluttered around his tongue. As Rosie came down from her high, Rob was rubbing his face over her stomach and up her chest, before capturing her lips in an exaggeratedly wild, passionate kiss she believed could have rivalled any porn scene she'd ever seen.

"How the fuck are you still clothed?" she asked, tugging at the hem of his t-shirt.

"Yeah, regretting that now." After helping Rosie pull the cotton up and over his head, Rob sat up and began the awkward struggle to rid himself of his jeans and underwear. He chucked them off the side of the bed, where they landed in a crumpled heap.

Rosie watched with reignited interest as Rob grabbed the foil square he'd set aside earlier and tore into it, then rolled the condom over his straining, leaking cock. However, instead of crawling back over her, he climbed off the bed and directed her to lie back sideways across the mattress.

Complying, she stifled a surprised squeal as he reached out and lifted her legs, sliding both hands under her ass as he pulled her to the edge of the mattress until she felt she might fall off the bed. The squeal shifted to a moan of approval as her legs were then guided over his shoulders and he finally slid inside her.

Rob's thrusts were deep, hard, and measured. Rosie had to admire his restraint. As it was, she could feel her next orgasm building, and she concentrated on clenching around him, trying to goad him into increasing his pace.

Instead, he picked Mack back up and switched him on again.

Rosie swallowed convulsively, unable to prevent herself from crying out as the vibrator was pressed against her still sensitive clit. This time when she clenched around Rob's cock, it was involuntarily.

"That's it," he praised with a strained, roughened voice, "come for me, baby. I'm not gonna hold out much longer."

"F-faster," her breathing hitched as her body teetered on the edge of another climax.

With a groan, Rob moved his hips quicker, the thrusts no longer as hard but just as deep. He leaned forward, almost bending Rosie in half in order to kiss her - not a position she thought she was flexible enough for, but the additional stretch of her muscles was not an unwelcome sensation.

"Fuck, I love you," he muttered against her lips.

The unexpected words, even though they'd exchanged them earlier, startled her orgasm from her. It ripped through her, somehow more intense than the one before it, and she was only barely cognisant of the sounds she was making as he continued to fuck her through it, quietly warning her he was coming as well, before his hips lost their rhythm and he stilled and groaned.

Her legs felt like jelly as Rob eased them down off his shoulders, and he helped her sit upright on the edge of the mattress. He took the condom, the wrapper, and the vibrator and left the bedroom, presumably to head into the bathroom which was just a couple more doors down the hallway. It took Rosie half a second to realise Rob had headed out there completely naked and heedless of the fact.

Then again, he was eye candy in every way possible and she supposed he knew it.

But where most sinfully attractive men she'd known were arrogant, he was genuine and sweet. She was lucky to have found him, and luckier still that he'd been patient while she had sorted herself out.

"What're you thinking so hard about?"

Rosie startled at the sound of Rob's voice as he carefully shut the bedroom door behind him. She smiled up at him. "How I'm not letting you go. Like, ever."

He grinned back at her and tossed her toy down onto the pile of crumpled clothes before bending over her to connect their lips in a sweet, chaste kiss. "I'm glad to hear it," he told her, cupping her jaw with one hand and smoothing his thumb over her cheek, " 'cos I'm not plannin' on letting you go, either."

Epilogue – Six Months Later

"So, here you go, leaving me again," Stefan accused playfully wrapping Rosie up in a huge hug. "I'm not holding a place for you anymore, just so you know."

She squeezed him and kissed his cheek. "As if you need me anymore," she argued as she pulled away from the embrace. "What with that insanely hot replacement you hired all of two minutes after I gave you my notice." She winked at him. "It's almost like you had him waiting in the wings."

A blush crept up his neck and face. "It was just good timing."

"That's gotta be a good sign, then, mate," Rob declared, swinging his arm over Rosie's shoulders. "Seein' as it's how you got this one to start with."

"Yeah, but I wasn't his type," Rose bantered back, smirking at Stefan. "But the Michael B. Jordan lookalike he's hired, on the other hand…" She snickered and jumped out of the way as Stefan moved to smack her arm.

"*Not* the reason I hired him."

"No, I know." She knew when to stop, not wanting to push the joke too far. "But you should definitely ask him out." As Stefan hesitated, opening his mouth to object, Rosie took pity on him and added, "I have it on good authority he'll say yes in a heartbeat."

She'd been sure to play wingman for Stefan and suss the new guy out while she'd been training him. It was the least she could do, considering all her friend-slash-employer had done for her.

"And Rosie's room's free now, so…" Rob waggled his eyebrows.

Stefan shook his head with a sigh. "You're both evil," he said, before tugging Rob in for a hug, giving him a couple of quick slaps on the back. "You look after my girl, RJ."

One year earlier, it would never have occurred to Rosie that one of her high school crushes might actually treat her like a sister, nor that she would have been overly impressed with the dynamic, but there she was, filled with warm, fuzzy feelings. Even more so when Rob emphatically assured their mutual friend that of course he would take care of her.

"I'm gonna miss the farm," she declared, slipping into the passenger seat of Rob's car.

"What? My apartment isn't good enough?" Rob teased as he slid into the driver's seat, turned the key and they listened to the engine rumble to life. "We can always visit. He's still my client. And my brother-in-law." He held his arm out over the back of her seat, as he shifted in his own to watch as he reversed out, ignoring the fancy screen in the console belonging to the reversing camera. "We're stuck with Stefan for life."

Even though they had been officially dating for six months, Rosie kept waiting for her anxiety to kick in and ruin everything. But whenever Rob said something offhand that reminded her of how effortlessly he thought of their life going forward as a pair, any niggling worries she had vanished without a trace.

As they left the crunch of the gravel for the hum of smooth bitumen, Rosie reached for Rob's hand; he rested them on his warm, denim-clad thigh. "I'm glad," she told him, and if she happened to be referring to more than just Stefan's ongoing presence in her life, she kept the thoughts private for the time being. She felt at peace, and nothing more needed to be said.

* * *

"Babe," Rob began a couple of weeks later, leaning against the doorway to the shared home office in the apartment which he'd insisted Rosie refer to as *theirs*.

She glanced up from her laptop, her jaw dropping to find him in a suit not dissimilar to the one he'd worn to Brennan and Jeff's wedding, or his sister's, for that matter. His hair was artfully styled back with gel, and his stubble was neatly trimmed. Just the sight of him dressed up like that had her pulse racing. It was a Saturday evening. They'd both been wearing casual attire the entire day. She didn't think they had any formal commitments. Or maybe they did and she had forgotten?

"What...?"

He chuckled - sounding sightly nervous to her ears- and shrugged. "I wanted to surprise you with a nice night out."

She glanced at the clock. It was still early. At least he appeared to realise she needed time to get ready. Shutting her laptop screen with a soft *snick*, she swivelled her chair around and aimed for coy. "Do I get to know where you're taking me?"

He shook his head. "Nope. That's part of the whole 'surprise' deal."

By that point in their relationship, Rosie knew that she wouldn't be getting any more information out of him than he was willing to impart. "Black tie?" she asked, looking his suit over while getting to her feet. The sweet and spicy scent of his aftershave tickled her nose as she neared him. It also never failed to spark her arousal, though she figured that was more likely the result of the combination of how handsome he was with how delicious he smelled, rather than the expensive cologne itself.

"Cocktail," he answered, smirking at her as though he could read her thoughts. "I'll probably ditch the jacket once we're there."

"Hmm," Rosie mused, smoothing her hand over the lapel, "pity. You know I love the suit."

"Yeah, well, you also love me naked," he waggled his eyebrows and pushed away from the doorframe, playfully swatting her butt, "and the feeling's definitely reciprocated."

"You gonna join me in the shower?"

He laughed and shook his head. "If I do we won't leave the apartment tonight. And we've got somewhere to be, so..." his sigh was rueful, "not this time, babe."

"Somewhere to be, huh?"

Rob laughed, the sound as rich and deep as usual. "That's all you're getting from me. Now scoot."

He wasn't usually so concerned with being on time, and the hint of tension in his shoulders had Rosie's brain whirring with possibilities. He wasn't going to propose, was he? They'd only been dating six months. That seemed improbable, especially for someone as methodical as Rob.

Curiosity piqued, she did as he requested. After showering and taking the time to shave her legs and underarms, she tamed her curls with the expensive spray her hairdresser had talked her into buying and meticulously applied her makeup. With how good Rob looked, there was no way she was going out looking anything less than glam.

Choosing a dress was difficult, though. Rob had said cocktail attire, but Rosie knew the suit he was wearing cost more than her first car had.

"Seriously, babe, you look hot in anything." Rob was seated on the edge of his – *their* - king size bed, cocking his head at her as she hovered inside the doorway of the walk-in robe with two dresses in hand. "Wear a hessian sack if that's what you're most comfortable in."

Snorting, Rosie held a black dress against her frame and examined herself in front of the full-length mirror, and then the turquoise one in front. Both were tea-length, flared from the waist down and fitted at the top – a style which flattered her curvaceous figure. She met his gaze in the reflection. "Is the blue too out there for where we're going?" With teardrop cut outs across the chest, it was tasteful, but gave just a hint of cleavage.

The turquoise dress was bright, and she liked wearing it around Rob. The first time she had, she'd noticed that the colour complemented his steely blue eyes...but, also, he'd been unable to keep his hands off her. It was a favourite for that reason.

He grinned at her reflection in the mirror, his thoughts likely similar to her own, and gave a minute shake of his head. "Nah, it's perfect."

Rosie had no reason not to trust his judgement. "This one it is."

He helped zip it up when she asked, kissing the back of her neck, and then led the way out of the apartment towards a waiting Uber.

176

* * *

"That looked like Dad's car," Rosie said, turning in her seat as their Uber came to a stop outside one of the Gold Coast's fanciest hotels. The car she was referring to had been parked on the road.

"Your dad drives a black Audi, Rose. There are a million of them here." He chuckled and opened his door, thanking the driver before he climbed out. She repeated the sentiment and met Rob on the other side of the car, where he took her hand and brought it up to his lips. "Shall we?" He still seemed a little anxious.

Giving him a strange look, she squeezed his hand and nodded. "Lead the way."

Instead of heading towards the restaurant within the hotel, he walked them off to the side in the direction of one the function rooms. Rob stopped Rosie in front of the closed door and swallowed roughly before he spoke.

"Okay, so, don't hate me," he said, but before she had a chance question why on earth she possibly could, Rob reached for the door handle and swung the large timber open. They were greeted with a loud proclamation of 'Surprise!' from the large gathering inside.

Rosie's jaw dropped as Rob ushered her further into the space. Wait staff wandered the area with trays of canapes and champagne. In the centre of the room, a large, circular table was set up, with an artfully displayed stack of paperback copies of her novel. There were balloons and fairy lights and, most notably, banners containing her book's image and words declaring the event her launch party.

Choked up, she turned to her boyfriend. "Launch party?"

When she had opted to self-publish over pursuing traditional publishing (mostly due to her desire to maintain creative control of her debut novel), Rosie had informed Rob she would soft launch the book. She had marketing strategies in place, of course, and had reached out to her connections in the media and the publishing world for assistance but hadn't planned on an official event. Instead, the day her paperback had gone live, she and Rob went out for dinner to commemorate the occasion privately. She'd insisted it was all she'd needed.

"You think you can fulfill one of your dreams and not have your friends and family celebrate the achievement?" Micah asked, stepping up to Rob's side and exchanging a friendly fist bump with him.

Rosie squealed and threw herself at her brother, wrapping her arms around him. "Oh my God!" She could feel her eyes welling with happy tears and was instantly glad to have chosen her waterproof mascara. "When did you fly in?" She hadn't seen him in *months*. Not since he'd moved to LA a week after Brennan's wedding. She pulled back and eyed him over. He was certainly more muscular than she recalled. It suited him. "Putting in time at the gym, huh?" There was something else in his expression. A sort of contentment that she couldn't quite name. "Dating?" She wondered aloud.

Micah laughed. "Aesthetic's the thing over there," he shrugged. "So, yeah, I've seen a lot of the gym lately. But, to answer your first question: I flew in yesterday. I couldn't miss this." There was genuine pride and warmth in his expression, even as she narrowed her gaze at how he sidestepped the question about his love life. "I'm so proud of you, Rosie," he beamed.

Her shoulders inched towards her ears. "It's just a smut book…"

"Stop it." That was her dad's voice, startling her as both her parents stepped up beside her brother. "Don't belittle your efforts, sweetheart."

"You've read it?" With wide eyes, she turned back to Micah, feeling her cheeks burn. "You *let him* read it?"

"Heavily redacted," Rob cut in, shaking Isaac's hand and leaning forward to kiss Rosie's mother, Meredith, on the cheek in greeting.

Things between Rosie and her mum remained stilted but had begun to thaw after Rosie had made the first move to bridge the gap. The fact that her boyfriend was an extremely attractive, successful lawyer with his own firm hadn't hurt, though it continued to rankle Rosie that appearances were still seemingly important to the older woman. It was as though she hadn't learned anything from Rosie's breakdown.

But Rosie was not letting it bother her. Not at the surprise launch party her boyfriend had arranged just for her. She directed her thoughts back to the actual conversation at hand.

"Well, that's something." Slowly, some of the tension in Rosie's shoulders dissolved. "Thinking of my parents reading...*that*..." she shuddered. "No thanks."

"Your father and brother are right, though," her mother spoke up. "This is quite an achievement, Rosemary. We're all proud of you."

There was still a world of hurt for them to work through, but Rosie swallowed roughly at hearing words her mother had once only reserved for Micah being directed at her. Her returning smile was watery. "Thank you."

Sensing the discussion was becoming a tad too heavy, Rob lightly grasped Rosie's elbow and apologised to her parents, explaining that he needed to take the guest of honour on the rounds of the room. Steadying her breathing, it was then that Rosie took in the sheer number of attendees. Liv and Grant surged forward to embrace her first, followed by Stefan, then Belinda and her wife, Fiona. Brennan and Jeff emerged from the crowd, too, hugging her tightly between them as they offered their own congratulations and words of support. Then it became a blur of names and faces; people she or Rob had worked with over time, acquaintances from Facebook and the like. Ultimately, the whole thing felt like an out-of-body experience.

"I can't believe you organised all of this," Rosie murmured against Rob's neck when she was able to steal a moment alone with him. And, to think before all of this, she'd thought the man couldn't be more perfect if he tried.

Rob's chest rumbled against her lips, since Rosie was snuggled right up against him. "I didn't overstep?"

"No," Rosie pulled back and beamed at him. "No. This is..." she waved a hand around the room, still finding the whole experience surreal. "This is beyond amazing, Rob." She chuckled. "And here I thought you were proposing."

He choked on the mouthful of champagne he'd just decided to sip, his face turning red. "*What?*" He cleared his throat, attempting to breathe. "Is...is that something you want?"

"What? Oh, God, no. I mean, not right now." They'd already agreed that neither of them wanted kids -the conversation they'd shared at the beginning of their relationship had melted into relief for the both of them- but she flashed back to Brennan's wedding and the fantasy she'd had about Rob being the sort of man (*the* man, in fact) with whom she had imagined exchanging vows.

She allowed her gaze to follow Rob's to where his best friend, Pete, stood with his wife, Rebecca. They were chatting with Micah, who was lapping up the attention. Pete's hands were glued to the swell of Bec's belly, the baby being the only thing either truly wanted to talk about, and Rob had confessed that he never wanted to be 'those people' as much as he liked the couple. Rosie hoped he didn't think marriage automatically meant an obligation to have kids. She would be certain to reassure him that her feelings on the matter hadn't changed.

Reaching down, she squeezed his hand. "Maybe one day, in the distant future, if you asked me to marry you…I wouldn't say no. But, y'know, still no on the kid front. Sorry not sorry; I'm keeping you all to myself. I'm still selfish like that."

Lips quirking upwards, he turned back to her with the same perpetual amusement he had always regarded her with, ever since their fateful meeting in the pine forest. "Maybe one day, in the not *too* distant future, I will ask then." He cast one last glance in Pete's direction and gave his head a shake before raising his glass to her. "But tonight is one hundred percent about you, and *only* you, babe."

Lifting her own glass and clinking it against his, Rosie smiled and took a celebratory sip. A year earlier she had been miserable, second guessing every single one of her life choices. She'd hated her career, had resented her mother and brother, and her love life had been dead on arrival. When she'd tossed out the cockamamie idea to write an article about former flames and missed connections, she never imagined her life would change so quickly from there.

Rosie had been looking for something fun. Something different to shake up the monotony. But what she'd found had been a whole lot more than that.

Was this where she thought her life would lead her? No. It was even better.

The opening beats of Lizzo's song, *Truth Hurts*, caught Rosie's attention, causing her to smirk to herself. She *had* needed something more exciting.

And she'd gotten it.

She'd gotten it all, and she couldn't have been happier.

* * *

Thank you so much for reading *Truth Hurts*. I really hope that you enjoyed it!

I'd love to hear what you thought of it at Goodreads or your preferred online retailer.

Reviews not only help make me a better writer, but they also help the algorithms that assist a book's online visibility and sales listings.

On the fence about leaving a review?

It's okay to leave a star rating and say nothing at all.

Thank you in advance for helping me out!

Happy Reading!

Neat

About the Author

Anita (A.N.) Verebes is a daydreamer and romance novelist. As a civil marriage celebrant, Anita makes a living telling other people's love stories and celebrating real romance! Also armed with a Bachelor of Education (Secondary), Anita is a qualified -but not practising- High School English teacher who loves to read anything she can get her hands on, including fanfiction. (And, yes, she's written her fair share of that, too.) Living directly between Queensland's sunny Gold and Sunshine coasts, Anita spends her days exploring the Great South East with her husband and their two rambunctious sons. When at home, she's also a slave to two cats and one very spoilt Great Dane X.

You can connect with me on:
🌐 https://anverebesauthor.wordpress.com
f https://www.facebook.com/ANVerebes

Subscribe to my newsletter:
✉ https://anverebesauthor.wordpress.com/newsletter_signup

Also by A.N. Verebes

A.N. Verebes writes Contemporary Romance. Light, feel-good, easy reads that scratch an itch...and turn up the heat!

Handle With Care

When Gemma Fox gets stuck in a lift with her celebrity crush, Everett Rhodes, she writes the whole encounter off as a fluke. However, life has other plans for both of them, and it changes everything.

You Can't Hurry Love

Sara Carlisle and Charlie Rhodes are complete opposites. Oil and water. Chalk and cheese. But, when their relationship turns from reluctant acquaintances to red hot lovers, they find it's good.

Really good.

What could possibly go wrong?

In a slow-burn, standalone romance that follows hot on the heels of *Handle With Care,* Sara and Charlie discover that you really can't rush romance.

www.ingramcontent.com/pod-product-compliance
Lightning Source LLC
Chambersburg PA
CBHW070319120726
47909CB00008B/2516